BOY ON A TRAIN

LESLIE MCADAM

Photograph of Kyle Sawyer by Cory Stierley

Cover design by Just Write Designs

Formatting by L. Woods LLC

THE ALL-AMERICAN BOY SERIES

Welcome to Merlot, CA, an idyllic all-American town in wine country where love is in the air, the boys are grown as fine as the wine and the town is a breeding ground for second-chances, weddings, and brand-new beginnings.

The All-American Boy Series gives you a taste of 15 of your favorite bestselling authors' brand new stories in this shared world experience. All books are standalone but may include cross-over in characters or scenes.

Grab a glass of wine, put your feet up and let us whisk you away to wine country.

Read them all now!

The Boy Next Door by Sierra Hill
Boy Toy by Poppy Parkes
The Boy Scout by Evan Grace
The Boyfriend Hoax by Emily Robertson
Boy Trouble Kaylee Ryan/Lacey Black
Celebrity Playboy by Kimberly Readnour
Backroom Boy by Marika Ray

Boy on a Train by Leslie McAdam
Bad Boy by K.L. Humphreys
Hometown Boy by Nicole Richard
That Boy by Remy Blake
The Boy She Left Behind by Stephanie Browning
About a Boy by Stephanie Kay
Lover Boy by Renee Harless
Saviour Boy by S.L. Sterling

Boy On A Train

My best friend Tate and I have plans. Big plans.

1. Get the hell out of Merlot, California.
2. Ride trains around the world.

Though I have a secret third entry on the list of things I want to do …

3. Tate Lemieux

But when my family gets a life-changing diagnosis just as I'm about to graduate, all my plans look like they'll go up in smoke.

Right when I finally get the chance to be with the boy I've always loved …

Will it end before it's even begun?

Boy on the Train is a standalone new adult friends to lovers romance from USA Today bestselling author Leslie McAdam full of sweet tension, fun banter & a side of family drama.

ONE

THE ANTI-BUCKET LIST

AUDREY

I f I had any idea today would be the day my life would change, I probably would've spat my gum out first.

But since I had no idea, I kept right on licking my blow pop, aiming for the bubblegum inside.

It was a normal Thursday afternoon, and I lay plopped on my stomach on my bed with the bedroom door open while Tate Lemieux watched me.

Platonically. Fully dressed. As friends.

"So, Audrey. Tell me what's on your list." Tate gazed at me with an expectant expression, as if I had any idea what he was talking about.

I didn't. "What list?" I said it loud enough so Dad could hear that Tate and I weren't sucking face from where he watched the Giants game in the den all the way down the hall.

See, Dad. Nothing to worry about. Boy in my room? No big deal.

A shudder ran through me from the memory of various lectures I'd received throughout my high school years to never be alone in my room with a boy if the door was closed.

Dad needn't have worried at all though, because Tate had never kissed me.

Even though I wished he would.

Despite the warnings, my dad probably had some weird psychic certainty that Tate had barely so much as held my hand, which accounted for me being able to spend so much time with him.

Which was a lot.

Every day Tate gave me a ride to and from Merlot High in a huge purple truck, carried my one-ton Statistics book to my class no matter how many times I told him I could carry it—and even though he didn't have that class with me—and spent lunch period feeding me catered gourmet food and Skittles.

He treated me like I was the most fascinating creature in town. Maybe all of Sonoma County and into Napa.

Evidence? Last Saturday night he ignored nonstop texts and come-ons from Jade Lopez, the most beautiful girl in school, in favor of a trip to Target to buy me a new toothbrush.

More evidence?

Almost every afternoon, Tate hung out with me from after school until dinnertime. We did our homework together then talked or watched Netflix until he headed home to his parents' huge, ranch-style house high atop the dusky green hills overlooking Merlot. He never stayed for dinner, even though my parents invited him most nights.

We've repeated this daily pattern since the middle of our sophomore year. But the lack of kissing meant we were just friends.

I mean, we must have been friends, right? Because if we were more than that, I'd know.

Right?

Not knowing drove me crazy.

I sucked hard on the watermelon blow pop, keeping myself

from the holy (and wholly satisfactory) bliss of biting into the bubble gum in the center, because once you did that, the flavor vanished in an instant.

It was infinitely more fun to draw it out.

I needed to savor these last days of high school since the amount of time till graduation was thinning out, and I didn't want to find that once I got to the end, the flavor had disappeared.

I glanced up at Tate sitting in my chair like a prom king. He was the most desired boy in school with his athletic build, golden-haired looks, old money, and cheeky charm. His appeal was of the stereotypical variety—he looked like an all-American boy from an eighties movie. Thankfully, all-American boys now came in more varieties and colors to choose from, with optional features. Tate just happened to be the one in my life.

Virtually every girl and quite a few of the boys wanted him, but he ignored them in favor of paying attention to me. And for the life of me, I couldn't figure him out.

Did he want me or not? Was he asexual? Did he not like *anyone*?

I was too scared to find out the answers to those questions, so I settled for not asking them. I didn't want to find out my crush on Tate only went one way.

I'd also been anxious about what would happen after graduation. Our plan was for not much to change. After this summer, Tate and I would keep going to class, hanging out, and perhaps not eating dinner together, but our venue would change to New York City. He'd study International Relations at Columbia. I'd start to build my tweedy, tailored empire at the Fashion Institute of Technology, my first choice school. We'd both leave town.

Leaving town would coincidentally save me from my underlying fear—peaking in high school. Being like those locals who never stopped talking about the past.

I wanted to live in the future, one with fashion and food and travel and ... Tate.

For now, though, my desires were simple: one kiss from Tate.

A *serious* kiss. No pecks on the cheek. I wanted a real kiss.

And yes, I wanted *him* to do it to *me*.

Don't be hating. I could take the initiative and kiss him, but I didn't want to. After all this ambiguity, I wanted to be sure he wanted me. I needed him to show me he liked me before I did anything stupid that wasn't reciprocated. Was that too much to ask? I didn't think so.

So, I did ask. Sort of.

On my last birthday a month ago, I blew out eighteen candles and wished for him to make the first move.

He didn't.

If he had, then I'd know for sure I wasn't misinterpreting any of our interactions, because for all I knew, even after all this time—*especially* after all this time—Tate just wanted to be friends. The uncertainty drove me to extra purchases of blow pops.

I might have a tiny candy addiction.

Still, sometimes I thought he saw me as *more*, especially when I caught his eyes on me. Like now, as he watched me suck this bright pink lollipop.

Pretending I didn't notice his laser-focused attention on me, I tossed a tendril of my long, spirally auburn hair over my shoulder, hoping he'd watch. I was maybe a wee bit vain about my hair, but I couldn't help it. I adored the compliments.

My hair didn't stay in place, though, falling back to where it had been.

As slyly as possible, I peeked at him through the curtain of my locks to see if the move worked.

It did. He noticed, judging by the way his mouth paused on an inhale, lips slightly open, breath stuttering to a halt. Of course his classically handsome face distracted me—tan, with a beautiful jawline and cheekbone ridges like the sharp-peaked hills around Sonoma. His blond, wavy hair was nothing to disparage, either—thick and mostly unruly. We locked eyes, and the world held its breath.

Does his attention mean what I think it means?

Every time I was about to conclude I'd systematically read our interactions all wrong for years and his interest in me was nothing beyond friends, he did something like this.

He made me feel wanted.

But as usual, we both blinked and re-situated, as if we'd been blocking a scene for a school play and now were starting over from the top. I pretended not to preen from his approval, although it warmed me from the inside, pinking my pale cheeks. He bluffed too, staring at his phone, as if he hadn't just gotten entranced watching me flip my hair. Everything went back to normal again.

That's how we roll.

It sucked monkey balls. Actually, I'd never sucked monkey balls—who had?—so perhaps it sucked like getting to the mushy, gross paper stick at the middle of a lollipop. *Yuck.*

"What list?" I repeated.

"I wanna make a list of what we're going to do when we're done with high school," he explained in his gruff voice.

Note: I *love* his rumbly voice.

"Like, a bucket list?"

He paused and glanced up from his phone. "No. I don't wanna call it a bucket list, because I'm not planning on waiting that long, and I'm not kicking the bucket early."

I turned over to my back and stared at my bedroom ceiling. Nothing to look at but ceiling, but this position meant I wasn't staring at Tate. "So it's an Anti-Bucket List?"

Then my eyes went to him.

Tate tilted his head from side to side, contemplating. "I see it as an organizational document to guide future decision-making." He sat back in my desk chair, scrolling on his phone, like he had a notes app open, but then he set it down and started riffling in my desk drawers. "So, I repeat. What do you wanna do after we graduate?"

Be with you. "How should I know?"

"You could start thinking about it."

I already know. I want to be with you. "Okay. Umm. Go to New York City."

He refrained from rolling his eyes. "You're such a dork sometimes," he said, his tone fond. "That's already on the list. What about when we aren't in school? We can travel on week-ends, holidays. Hell, maybe I'll talk you into ditching class or taking a semester to study abroad. We can do *whatever* we want." The way he growled out "whatever" sounded sexual, and it made me shiver. That shiver was nowhere near platonic.

I'd never done *that*, but I didn't want to put *that* down on the Anti-Bucket List. I had no idea if he had, and I didn't want to find out, because it wouldn't have been with me. I clung to his other words. "Can't we already do whatever we want? We're both adults."

"And get written up for truancy and hauled before the principal? Or have to explain what we're doing to our parents? Nah, no thanks. I'm talking about after we leave Merlot. When we're really free." He reached out to touch my hand. His long, lean fingers felt warm on my skin.

He moved his hand back almost too fast for me to register the contact and kept talking. "My mom says we need to make plans, or we won't live. I don't wanna wake up at forty-five having never experienced half the things I wanted to do. I want to go on the Orient Express and learn to sail in Denmark and climb mountains in Argentina. As a famous pirate said, if we don't have a personal map, we'll never find the treasure."

I sat up and narrowed my eyes at him. "No pirate said that."

"True." He grinned, and I laughed, reached over, and shoved his shoulder. He wasn't that close, and my shove wasn't very hard. I tried not to linger on the muscly shape of his upper body.

"*You're* the dork."

Tate was always planning. And doing. He'd show up with my favorite pizza on a Saturday afternoon or haul me to the BART station to go to the city for an indie movie. I think he liked riding the Bay Area Rapid Transit.

Or maybe he just liked trains.

He also brought me presents all the time. A cute new pair of knee-high socks with taco cats on them to wish me luck before an important test. Strawberry-flavored KitKats from Japan because of my obsession with candy. Pink Himalayan salt—that he got in the Himalayas—because, yeah. That was what Tate was like.

And why he confused me as to whether he was my friend or more than friends.

Constant gifts equaled more-than-friend behavior. Right?

God, he made me feel stupid sometimes. Not by anything he said—and he never belittled my intelligence—but because I couldn't figure him out.

My dad called him William Randolph Hearst—Hearst's mother took him to Europe at age ten, which influenced the later construction of Hearst Castle in San Simeon—because he said Tate was the spoiled boy whose parents dragged him every-where. I usually argued back that Tate had brothers, so he couldn't be a Hearst, who was an only child. That argument went nowhere.

Tate remained on his Anti-Bucket List, dragging me from my thoughts. "Start easy. Where do you want me to take you shopping?" He licked his lips, and my brain stumbled to a stop wondering what it would be like to lick *his* lips.

"Oh. Lemme think."

As I contemplated, I sucked my lollipop, getting dangerously close to the flavor-laden gum in the center. I pretended to think about the future since I was really just wondering what Tate tasted like. But after a moment I had a few things to rattle off.

"I want to buy gold sparkly Doc Martens in London. Wouldn't those look amazing with a bouclé jacket and jeans? And go to F.A.O. Schwartz in New York City for a limited-edition Barbie. If they have one that looks like me, all the better."

"Uh huh," he muttered, scribbling these in a small memo notebook decorated with cats that he'd found in my desk. "Get an Audrey Barbie in NYC. Anything else?" He grinned. "You know I love going with you for retail therapy."

He actually did. I'd never met a guy more willing to hang out while I tried on shoes. He usually encouraged me to purchase *both* pairs of shoes that I liked, not pick one. Once, he even returned to the store to buy a pair I didn't have enough money for and gave them to me as a present.

I should marry him just for that. For a brief moment, I imagined what it would be like to wear a white dress and walk down the aisle to Tate wearing a tuxedo, his blond hair and blue eyes shining in the sunlight.

Of course, not at age eighteen.

Or before I knew what he was like when he was naked.

Or before I confirmed he liked me *like that*.

"Any other shopping? Or other places to visit?" He asked this as if all I needed to do was just say what I wished and I could have it.

"All the Harry Potter filming sites in the UK. Venetian glass in Italy. A real Fabergé egg. A meat pie in Australia."

"Meat pie?"

"I heard they're good." I shrugged.

"Any other food?"

"Sushi in Japan. The more challenging, the better. I want tentacles."

The serious look on his face as he concentrated on the page, recording my comments, made my heart swell. But all he said was, "Got it."

"Ooh! I know!" I scrambled to the edge of the bed and faced him. "I've always wanted to ride trains."

He glanced up from where he was writing. "Why trains?"

"They're the most civilized form of transportation. I mean, besides private jet, I assume. You can get up, walk around, sleep, have a nice meal, knit, paint, read a book, look out the window. Freedom and independence without the responsibility of driving. Plus, they're romantic." I hoped I didn't blush.

"Alright," he said. Then he looked up. "Wait. You don't paint or knit."

"That's not the point. I *could.*"

"True. Okay, what else?"

I was getting worked up now. "Well, if we wanted to ride a train in every continent or every country or every kind of train, that could pretty much keep us busy the rest of our lives. It's perfect!"

Oops. I hoped he didn't pause at my use of the word "we." But it would be us doing these things together, right?

Why haven't we kissed yet?

"Sure. Do you want to travel by any other method? Blimp? Sidecar? Paddleboat?"

I bit the inside of my lip, still hung up on the train thing. "We *could* walk in the Black Forest of Germany."

He smirked. "So, it's either take a train or walk. No, like, rent a *car* in Germany. You know there's the Autobahn, right?"

"That's expected, though. No. I don't want to take normal transportation if we can help it. Let's go by train. Or walk. Especially in enchanted forests. I read an article about inns in that area and thought it sounded dreamy."

He tilted his head. "Are all your travel ideas dreamy?"

I wasn't blushing. Not at all. "Maybe. The world's full of pretty things, right? I want to see them."

He took more notes, then glanced up at me. I reached over and brushed a lock of his hair behind his ear. Then I realized I'd touched him.

He stilled. I pulled back and hastily opened my mouth. "I can't believe you aren't fighting me on any of these," I said, and winked. "You make me feel like we can actually do them."

"Of course. We can do anything." And his wide smile blew me away. "You're George Bailey in *It's a Wonderful Life,* and we're planning your trip around the world. I want to give you everything you want."

Okay, first, he knew that was my favorite movie, since he'd seen it three times with me.

Second, I melted at the sincere look on his face. Tate's nickname should've been Fairy Godfather, because he was the best at making wishes come true. He never said something I wanted was dumb or that I wouldn't be able to get it or shouldn't have it. He only asked, how do I give it to you?

So, again, why didn't he have a girlfriend?

Or more accurately, why was I not that girlfriend? Because if we were dating, we'd be out the door. We'd leave Merlot and do things, both of the sexy variety and also the general, doing-more-with-our-lives variety.

The thought passed through my brain that he was gay, and his questions were just a friend thing. That I'd misinterpreted everything all along.

That thought made me irrationally pissy, so I shoved it aside.

"What's on *your* Anti-Bucket List?" I asked. "Where do you want to go?"

"Wherever you are," he answered immediately.

I shoved him gently on the shoulder again. *Mmmm, solid.* "I'm serious."

"So am I."

"You're impossible."

He raised his eyebrows. "I believe the term is, 'handsome.'"

God was he ever handsome. Tate radiated confidence in a playful way.

I ignored him and went back to our original topic. "It might be simpler to buy one of those round-the-world plane tickets or get a Eurorail pass. Can we take everything else off the list and just see where those would take us? Because that's it." I kicked my feet excitedly. "I want to ride a train. With you. Everywhere. And travel the world without ever driving anywhere."

"No taxis?"

"Well, we don't have to be perfect," I admitted. "We can rely on taxis in some places. And I'd like to take one of those things in Thailand. What are they called?"

"What am I, *Wikipedia*?"

"You have this weird mind for geography and history facts."

"True. They're rickshaws. Or *tuk tuks*, depending on if they're motorized."

"See? You are *Wikipedia*. How do you know these things?"

He shrugged. "My mom took me there."

Of course he'd been to Thailand. He'd been everywhere, unlike me.

His mother, Sandra Lemieux, was a famous wine country caterer who hunted around the world for inspiration. She took private lessons from renowned chefs in other countries, arranged for imports of special ingredients only she had access to, and generally exposed him and his brothers to the entire world.

Meanwhile, I'd never been to Disneyland, which was in the same freaking state.

Pathetic, huh?

But my life was way different than his. Tate had piles of brothers. I had no siblings whatsoever. His dad ran some finance business. My dad was the fire chief, not the go-to caterer for every fancy soiree in the Valley. And unlike his globetrotting mother, as of late, my mom had been sick. She'd taken a leave of absence from her teaching job, although we didn't know her diagnosis other than fatigue.

Still, Tate Lemieux knew my dreams. He knew I wanted to go places and do things and that I had this itch in my soul. The fact that Tate took the time to write my dreams down mattered, because he was the kind of guy who could get these things done.

If I were going to fall in love, I'd fall in love with him.

I bit my sucker, getting to the gum, and started chewing.

He unlocked his phone. "Shit. I have to go home. Pick you up tomorrow morning for school?"

"Yeah," I said, sitting up on the edge of the bed as he stood and gathered his backpack, sliding his phone into the back pocket of his jeans. "Wanna stay for dinner? At least it's not pork chops."

"No, thanks." Tate grinned. "Mom wants to try a new recipe."

"Of course she does," I muttered.

"You can come by—"

I held up a hand. "No. Dad already started dinner."

"Okay," he conceded. "Another time."

He ripped out the page from the kitty cat notebook and folded it, also pocketing it. Then he paused before he turned to leave, looking down at me. He normally just smiled and waved.

The expression on his face now was not something I'd seen before. Unless I was imagining it, his expression was *heated*.

He leaned over, and his big eyes studied mine for a moment. With a finger under my chin, he tilted up my face—

And kissed me.

My door stood wide open. My parents could walk by at any time.

But his soft lips touched mine.

Fast.

This quick peck had no choice but to be memorable, since it was our first kiss, a closed-mouth and speedy caress. So fast I didn't know what he tasted like. I still had the bubble gum in my mouth when he was done.

I was so startled, I almost didn't kiss back, and I forgot to close my eyes. I was sure they were huge.

His finger traced my jaw, and he hoisted his backpack over one shoulder. "See you tomorrow?"

The only thing I could do was nod, my brain on the fritz. He turned, walked down the hall, called goodbye to my parents, and let himself out before I could unfreeze.

I brought my fingers to my lips and touched where his lips had been, wondering what it all meant and knowing it was the sweetest kiss I'd ever had.

It made me want more. Of him. Of his lips. Of our dreams. Of *everything*.

But I didn't know if that could ever come true. Maybe my

dreams were just something written on kitty cat paper and shoved in a pocket, never to happen.

"Dinner in a half hour!" my dad called.

I straightened my face and threw out my gum.

No matter what, my relationship with Tate had just changed.

And I couldn't wait to find out how.

TWO

THE MOBILE LIVING ROOM

TATE

Slightly stunned and blinking, I shut her front door and stumbled out to my truck, my head spinning, my senses full of the candy-sugar scent of Audrey Staunton. Her words echoed in my brain.

That's it. I want to ride a train. With you. Everywhere.

I glanced back at the house.

God, I love her. I really fucking love her.

It physically pained me to spend any time away from her. I had to force myself to go home every day, because if I didn't, I'd never leave. She was my addiction.

A probably unhealthy addiction, but I didn't care. I just wanted to be with her. As days passed, it became harder and harder to hide my feelings for her—if I ever hid them well to begin with.

I'd had it bad for Audrey ever since we met our freshman year of high school. My parents put me in private school for elementary and middle school, but I talked them into letting me go to public high school like my brothers before me.

Audrey sat in front of me that first day in math class, twirling her ringlets around her index finger and generally driving me to distraction. She dressed like the schoolgirl she was, with knee-high socks and Mary Jane shoes, short skirts, and tailored button-down shirts, long hair swinging behind her as she walked. She somehow nailed the look so it wasn't nerdy, but rather innocently sexy. Dark academia. Like she lived in the hot version of *Dead Poets Society*.

She loved tweed coats and cuffed pants and newsboy hats and wanted to design her own clothes in a similar style. With her beauty and style, no wonder she was noticeable. If she deigned to give you her attention, you'd die happy. Or at least I would.

Audrey was simply the most attractive girl I'd ever seen—always had been. But beyond her looks, I loved how much she cared about her family. And the variety of her interests—eating world cuisine, sampling every single form of candy ever made, repeat-watching *Peaky Blinders*. Spending the afternoon planning our future together engraved her even deeper upon my heart.

As much as I fantasized about grabbing her and shoving my tongue down her throat, that wasn't the way to make her like me. For almost four years, my tactic had been to go achingly slow, hoping she'd want me anywhere near as much as I wanted her.

For years, I'd thought she only wanted to be friends. But lately it had seemed like she'd been flirting. The way she'd tossed her hair just now. *God.*

Maybe I did it wrong, though. Maybe my kiss sailed in from nowhere, judging from the surprise in her eyes when I pressed my lips to hers. I couldn't kiss her longer, though. Couldn't risk Chief Staunton seeing us tangling tongues. Not when I'd overheard his keep-the-door-open lectures before. I wouldn't do that to her.

I got in the MLR, my Mobile Living Room—so named

because the bench seats of my oversized Barney-purple truck could probably hold a dozen people—and started the engine.

That girl had started my internal engine long ago. *Fuuuuck.*

Shifting into reverse, I backed away from her house. Her parents, Tim and Denise Staunton, were the second owners of a 1970s tract home with a two-car garage and a lawn mowed short in front. It still had the original avocado green and harvest gold kitchen appliances. Amazing that stylish Audrey came from a complete time warp. Or maybe that explained why she wanted to update historical clothes for today.

I drove along the valley, then turned and climbed the vineyard-covered hills. Oak trees and pines dotted the landscape, breaking up the neat lines of the grapes, which were laced with bright yellow mustard flowers. Soon, I'd have a view of all of Merlot.

But I ignored the scenery. Marring my replay of our first kiss was an increasingly sinking sensation in my gut.

She hadn't kissed me back, and I kept debating whether I'd fucked up. I hoped I hadn't.

When I came to a stop sign, almost home, the silence in my truck startled me. I chuckled. I was so distracted, I'd forgotten to turn on any music. As usual, I'd only thought about her.

I'd put off kissing Audrey for so damn long because she was too important. She needed a forever guy—and I was all-in—but I didn't want to push her before she gave me a signal she was ready.

That didn't stop my subconscious making her star in all my dirty dreams, though.

I wasn't biding my time until she spread her legs for me. Nothing like that. I just was genuinely okay with taking it slow.

Because we had all the time in the world. There was no other girl for me. Period.

Although I was getting pretty antsy to kiss her again. And maybe do more, if she wanted to.

And therein lies the problem.

I made my way home, parked in the six-car garage, and strolled inside, the roll-top door shutting behind me. My parents' house smelled like butter, potatoes, and lemony chicken, mixed with vanilla and sugar. Home.

Entering the kitchen, I threw my backpack down on a bar stool and went to the fridge for a drink.

My mom turned around from her station at the island counter where she iced cookies. Mom had a blonde bob and wore a crisp chambray shirt over jeans. Her apron said *Lemieux Catering.*

"Hi, Tate. How's Audrey?" Mom asked, giving me a quick peck on the cheek as I passed.

My brother Perry didn't turn around, continuing to stir something in a copper pot on the stove. Staring at his face was like looking in the mirror in two years.

He loved food almost as much as she did and was always trying recipes with her. At twenty, his metabolism was high enough—plus he played enough club soccer—to keep the rich food from showing on his waist.

"You mean his girlfriend?" Perry snorted, then reached for the salt.

"Shut up," I said, gulping a cold glass of water. I dug out my phone and checked for any texts from Audrey. None.

I've got it bad.

My mom grinned. "I know you aren't telling me to shut up."

I snorted when I realized my words could be misconstrued. "God, no, Mom. Not you. I'm talking to that tool over there." I pointed my cell phone at Perry.

"Boys." She clamped her lips together, suppressing a smile.

"She's fine, by the way." Audrey was way more than fine, but there was no way I'd let my mom know that.

"Are you dating or no?" Perry looked over his shoulder.

"No." I managed to not say it like a question. He'd asked me before, and I usually answered with more certainty.

I mean, were we dating? I'd never asked her out. I just hung out with her. I did things for her.

But I barely touched her because I needed to be very careful with her.

"So, you won't mind if I ask her out?" he asked breezily, and I growled low in my throat.

"Perry!" Mom's eyes flashed fire at him. "Don't provoke your brother."

"It's literally my job to provoke my brother," he insisted, laughing hard into the copper pot. "Forgotten middle brother needs to assert himself sometimes."

"Who's the middle brother?" My oldest brother Bert walked in, a clone of my dad, with darker hair than mine.

I drew the best straw for names. My brothers were named after our grandfathers. Not sure where Mom got the name Tate, but I'd take it over Perry or Bert.

"Me, asshole," Perry said without heat.

"Language," Mom said, shaking her head and reaching for more frosting. But I knew it didn't bother her.

In this house, we never censored ourselves. Mom focused only on important things like avoiding broken bones and ensuring we all went to the dentist. She'd let go of micro-control a long time ago. Our only house rule was, "don't swear where Grandma can hear."

Actually, there were a few other rules, namely, "don't splash Mom in the pool," and "don't pee on the floor." Every rule had been broken multiple times, by just about everyone.

Also, in other news, my parents were the coolest.

"Need any help?" I asked her to be polite but wanted to escape to my room.

"I'm fine, thanks, hon. What about you? Are you getting excited about graduation? Everyone's coming, you know."

"Can't wait." My tone was distracted because my phone vibrated, and I checked it hoping it was Audrey. But it was this girl, Jade.

Jade: Have you seen? Mr. Peterson posted the grade on our final project

Me: No

She and I had been paired for a Drama project, and ever since she got my number, she hadn't stopped texting me. I tried to respond as little as possible.

Jade: We got an A-!!

Me: Awesome

Jade: I know, right?

Jade: <celebration gif>

My mom continued talking, a wistful tone to her voice. "You don't know how much it means to me and your dad that you chose our alma mater. You're going to love it in New York City. It's the center of the universe. The arts. The culture. The restaurants. The food. All those interesting neighborhoods."

And Audrey coming with me. If she'd chosen studying in Anchorage, I'd have gone there with her instead.

Jade: See you tomorrow!!

I didn't bother to respond, because I didn't want to encourage her to keep texting me. I didn't know why she wouldn't leave me alone.

"Something makes me think I'll wake up one day in New York to you and Dad lurking in my living room." I reached around my mom and stole a cookie.

"Hmmm. Maybe." My mom looked at the clock on the oven and shooed me away. "Have you done your homework?"

I had, but I had a date with my computer. "I'll be in my room." I refilled my water, grabbed my backpack, and went down the hall, leaving my brothers and mom talking about recipes.

When I got to my room, I opened my laptop, pulled out the Anti-Bucket List from my pocket, and started Googling. Let's say we started with London. Audrey needed a passport, so I researched application requirements. Then she'd be able to jet off as easily as me.

I created a Google doc with links for fun things I knew she'd like—classic sights and special restaurants. Eventually, I had a working plan to spoil her with everything she'd ever wanted.

That was the easy task on my to-do list.

But I had another one.

I checked the time on my laptop. Still a few minutes before dinner.

That peck on her lips? Not enough. But I didn't know what I was doing in the bedroom. At all.

Which was my deep dark secret.

It embarrassed me and was another reason why I'd put off touching Audrey. For years, I'd paid attention only to her, which meant I hadn't fooled around with anyone else. I'd only ever kissed other girls in junior high, so I'd had a long dry spell. Very long.

I was a virgin.

Pathetic.

I needed sex education. Sure, Mrs. Sanchez's Health class gave me basic information, and my parents were never shy about answering questions. But I didn't want answers to the *mechanics* of how to have sex. I wanted answers of how to have *good* sex. How to make it amazing for her.

I'd pay a lot of money for a how-to guide for being the best in bed. Something that would avoid trial and error. Audrey didn't deserve me fumbling. I wanted confidence. And to take care of her. And to, well, be a total sex god.

The trouble was, I had no idea how to do that.

Even worse, I needed to start with the basics, because my kissing technique needed work. Today being a classic example. So, I had some research to do. But where?

The way I saw it, my choices sucked.

Choice one, I could watch porn. But it was unlikely to tell me the truth, and from what I'd seen, I didn't think Audrey had a big-dick nipple-clamp fake-secretary kink. Or whatever.

Although if she did, that would be interesting.

Setting aside that digression ...

Choice two, I could ask Bert and Perry. Ditto as to the problem of them not telling me the truth. Oh, they'd get around to it eventually after telling me that I had to suck her toes first or something. Assholes. Same for asking friends at school, but they were a worse choice since I didn't trust them not to blab to everyone that I was a virgin. So, no.

Or choice three, I could ask the internet. There had to be some websites teaching guys how to do this right. Right?

Information was just the first problem, though. Because once I had said info, how did I put it to use? I couldn't practice on anyone but Audrey, which was inconvenient when I wanted her to be the object of my sex godliness.

An itchy feeling crawled on my skin. I had to figure this out. I had to be the best at this. For her.

"Dinner! Tate!"

"Coming!" I called. Then I snickered.

I hoped I'd be coming soon enough.

After dinner, I returned to searching on my laptop, hoping to find resources to help me not be a virgin.

To be clear, I realize I can't lose my virginity on the internet—I needed another person, not my own hand.

Much to my not-surprise, the internet didn't want to help me. Either the articles came straight from health class, scaring the fuck out of me about pregnancy and STDs—not the way to entice you to get your sexy on with your would-be girlfriend—or they were clickbait that told me nothing. Like, *25 Ways for Her to Give You Good Head*. Or *Sixteen Places to Fuck Outside before You Die*.

These how-to articles were geared more toward women than men. Sexism, much? They weren't at all for beginners like me.

Okay, maybe I copied the link to that second one to our Google doc.

Was it stupid that I wanted to make love to Audrey? I wanted her to feel sexy and loved and to know how I felt and—hell—to come. I wanted to find the female orgasm. Was that too much to ask?

After a few more internet searches, I gave up. It was late, and we had school tomorrow, but that didn't stop me from seeing what was up with my favorite porn site.

My cursor hovered over a thumbnail featuring an actress with long, curly auburn hair and slim pale legs. I clicked on it and found the post with the video. She resembled a certain someone I was in love with.

Shoving down my boxers and reclining in bed, laptop next to me, I knew how I'd be ending tonight's research.

But when it came to getting my sexy on for real, I just wished I knew what I was doing.

So it could be special for her.

THREE

POPCORN AND PORK CHOPS

AUDREY

Ever since I met him, talking with Tate had always been as easy as petting a dog—both he and I liked it, and we had no incentive to stop.

It wasn't easy today.

Right now, the last period before lunch, the handsome guy occupied the desk behind me in English, pen in hand, taking up too much space compared to what he'd been given. Tate's long legs extended into the aisle on either side and crowded up close to me, feet in black Chuck Taylors under his dark jeans. He could hook his feet on the metal chair legs and pull me to him. But he didn't have to touch me or make a move to affect me.

I could *feel* him. He wasn't doing anything except sitting behind me while the teacher droned on, but I sensed his presence, his eyes on me like he'd caught me in an invisible woven filament net and was reeling me in.

Because now I knew. I *knew* something was up with him, or rather, between him and me.

He kissed me.

That meant he wanted to be more than friends. *I* wanted to be more than friends. We secretly agreed.

I think.

No, I knew. He wouldn't have kissed me otherwise. Tate didn't see me as only his friend.

Hallelujah.

But this knowledge made me flustered.

Because Tate was watching me.

I didn't know what to do with my hands, my body, my thoughts. I did my best to sit still, but even that felt unnatural. The kiss magnified the significance of every moment.

Each move I made was studied, like an actor on stage. I felt overly self-conscious. The simplest of actions required more thought than ever before—tucking my pleated skirt under myself as I sat, sliding my bag under my chair, picking up my pen, raising my hand. I did my best to participate like always, although my thoughts on *The Handmaid's Tale* were on the fritz.

I needed to talk to him.

When he picked me up this morning in the MLR, I'd run out and opened the passenger door before he could turn off the engine and come up to our front door, which he'd do if I wasn't waiting for him, because he was a charming gentleman. I took a deep breath and clambered into the cab, not knowing what to expect.

What I received was his usual crooked smile and an iced latte with three sugars and a dash of cinnamon. "Morning. Got you this."

"Thank you." Did I lean over and kiss him? Did I say something? *Help.* "How early did you get up to get this?"

"It's no biggie," he said as always. He never answered my questions about the lengths he went to for my gifts, but he had to budget time for getting himself ready, waiting in line at the coffee shop, driving to my house, and still making it to school on time.

Again, why has some girl not snapped him up? *He's incredible.*

Then my skin tingled.

It was me. *I* was the girl in the process of snapping him up, which made this whole day different than any that had come before.

I wanted to climb into his lap. But with no clues from him that anything was different, I behaved as usual, pretending there'd been no kiss. I yawned and smiled and sat in the passenger seat of the MLR about a mile from him at the wheel, drinking my iced coffee, lost in my thoughts.

The ride to school was quieter than normal, although we were often less than animated first thing in the morning. He played our school playlist—songs the exact length of the drive to school, four and a half minutes.

It had taken us months to create the playlist, doing our best to get the songs down to the second, so we didn't spend any extra time sitting in the car for a song to finish or starting a new one that we wouldn't hear until after school.

A dumb game, sure, but it was the kind of thing he and I liked to do. Today was "Born this Way," although that needed ten more seconds to make it long enough. Tate knew this, so he started Lady Gaga ten seconds into the drive.

After bopping along, we'd arrived at school and split for our individual classes.

But now? It was almost lunch, which we always shared.

I didn't want this to be awkward. I just wanted him to be mine.

Tate wasn't the first boy I'd ever kissed. I'd kissed Court Thompson on a dare at a party, and I'd been to a few dances with boys besides Tate in my freshman and sophomore years. But after we started hanging out in earnest, it became automatic that he'd take me to homecoming or prom. As friends.

No wonder everyone thought we were dating. From the outside world it seemed like we were. I didn't want to broadcast that our first kiss had been only yesterday.

But I had to sort this out.

———

The bell rang, and we walked outside to the picnic tables. No cafeteria food for us. Tate's mom always made us a catered lunch. Today it was cold noodles in these adorable takeout boxes and spring rolls with dipping sauce. Being with Tate meant causing a healthy dose of lunch-envy in others. Not that I minded. It was yummy, and his mom was the best.

After we sat down and started eating, he asked, "How was math?"

As if this were a normal day.

"It was fine," I started, and opened my mouth to ask more. Like,

Why did you kiss me?

Do you like me like that?

Can we kiss for real?

But we were interrupted when Sam came and sat down beside us.

"Hey, guys! Wanna sign my yearbook?"

"Sure," Tate said, suppressing a sigh that only I noticed.

After we scribbled in Sam's book, a line formed. No joke. While we signed yearbooks, Jade Lopez sat down on the other side of Tate, too close. I wanted to scratch her eyes out, but I was above that.

So, I only thought about it.

Jade's dark hair lay in neat waves, not all crazy and spirally like mine. And she wore the trendiest things she could find—not my collegiate clothes inspired by *Raiders of the Lost Ark* and *Brideshead Revisited.*

Tate seemed to like what I wore, and he seemed to not want to talk to Jade. He scooted near me so his thigh pressed against mine, and my heart warmed even more for him.

Like there was any more room in there for him. He already took up my entire heart.

"Tate, do you want to come over tonight?" Jade asked, squeezing his forearm.

Was she serious? Tate was mine.

Maybe.

"No," he said. "I'm hanging out with my brothers and watching the game."

Her hand trailed up his arm. "You could watch it at my house."

"No, it's a thing we all do. I watch it with them." He reached over and put a hand on my thigh. He'd never done that before.

I found a secret space in my heart he hadn't already occupied and shoved him in there.

"Oh, too bad." Her bored voice had a wistful undertone.

What was her game? Asking out my, uh, boyfriend.

Was he my boyfriend?

God, I needed to talk to him, but other kids came over, including my best friend Wren Namuang, whose calculating eyes took in how I was plastered to Tate's side. "Hey, wanna meet me at the diner after school?" I asked.

"Can't," Wren said. "I've got piano. What about Saturday?"

"Yeah, I can do it then." I pulled out my phone and texted her from under the table.

Me: Lots to tell you

Her phone pinged, and I could see her hands flying under

the table. Thankfully, no one paid attention to us as Jade blabbered on about something.

Wren: Has something changed with you and Tate? He couldn't keep his hands off the back of your chair in class and now he's all touchy with you

Me: He kissed me

Wren looked down at her phone, then up at me, blinking. She got a wry look on her face and tilted her head while her chestnut eyes evaluated me like I was a puzzle she was trying to figure out. Finally, she texted,

Wren: He hasn't before?

Me: Nope

Tate turned toward me, a glorious smile on his face. "Hey, are you two texting?"

"Yeah," I admitted.

He laughed. "Okay. You know you're sitting right there. You could talk."

I shrugged, unable to come up with a good excuse.

"Fine," he said. "Don't let me stop you."

Then my phone pinged.

Wren: Well, fucking finally

And she gave me the biggest grin.

Wren: I'd high five you ... but that's a little obvious

My fingers ran over the screen of my phone.

Me: It was just a quick kiss

Me: My parents were home

Wren: But you guys have gone out all the time

Me: That was just as friends

She shook her head, her fingers moving fast.

Wren: All those times you've been to SF with him, it was just as a friend?

Me: Yeah. He barely held my hand before

Wren: What took you guys so long?

Me: I didn't even know if he liked me.

Her hand flew to her hip as she glared at me. Then the message came a moment later.

Wren: Are you serious? Of course, he likes you. He's always had the biggest heart-on for you

I giggled.

"What?" Tate asked, his forehead on my shoulder.

I shivered.

"Nothing," I said at the same time as Wren.

Me: Heart-on?

Wren: That's him. Also, Jade will die when she finds out he kissed you

Me: Ugh. Don't mention that viper. She won't leave him alone

Wren: I can see. Don't worry. He only has eyes for you

That made me feel better. Wren gathered her bag. "Gotta head to my locker." She gave Jade evil eyes, blew me a kiss, and took off.

Yep. That was why she was my best friend.

Jade left after pouting that Tate wouldn't do something else with her. I shoveled in two final mouthfuls of noodles and finished lunch. All the interruptions meant I had no chance to talk to Tate about personal stuff until school was over.

And I was a ball of nerves by the end of the day.

Two periods later, when the bell rang, I met him outside my class, trying not to wring my hands, and walked with him to his truck.

"Are you coming over?" I asked.

"Yeah." He took my Stats book from me. "If that's okay."

"Of course. We need to study for this Government final on Monday."

"Cool," he said, and when we got to the truck, I climbed in, wondering how to bring up that kiss.

Or—better yet—how to set aside time to kiss some more.

My dad knew something had changed between Tate and me. That was the only explanation. He kept pacing up and down the hallway past my room. He normally sat in the living room with my mom watching old episodes of *The X-Files*. But he must have figured us out, because he was jumpy.

Since we were under surveillance, Tate and I didn't even try to move near each other. At least, I didn't try to kiss him, and he didn't try to kiss me.

And the tension drove me utterly bananas.

I'd always known that Tate was a beautiful specimen of a boy. His T-shirt molded to his body today, clinging to his defined biceps and broad chest and filling me with want.

But with my dad hovering over us, I gave up trying to do anything kissy-kissy and instead focused on homework.

"Have you started studying for Government?" I asked. We had the same teacher, but in different periods.

"Yeah, I have, actually. It's almost as bad as History with how many dates we need to know. I made flash cards. Want me to make you a copy?"

I shook my head. "No, don't go to that trouble. But we could use them together and study."

He nodded and pulled a neat stack of index cards out of his backpack, then removed the rubber band and handed the cards to me. "Quiz me."

I read the first one out loud. "When did the Cuban Missile Crisis begin?"

"October 16, 1962."

"Good." I flipped to the next one. "You're always good at dates."

Tate bit his lip and grinned around it. "Wanna go on one with me?"

My hands shook, and I dropped all the cards. I breathed, "What?"

He reached down to pick them up, then peered up at me. "A date. You know, like, go somewhere and do something. Do you want to go on one with me on Sunday? I have family shit tomorrow."

His face was adorable, simultaneously earnest and steeling himself for me to reject him.

"Smooth," I said, recovering my voice. "Smooth transition. I give it a solid A."

"Is that a yes? We can go wherever you want."

I nodded and smiled, warmth blooming over my skin. "It's a yes. I want to go on a date with you." I couldn't help but tease him. "Then we *really* can see if you're good at dates—"

"I can only hope—"

"I meant for Government class." I winked.

"Oh," he said. "The only way I get good at them is to practice."

"So you aren't *Wikipedia*?"

"Nope. Want me to quiz you?"

My dad walked down the hall another time, whistling. I couldn't tell the tune. Then he ducked his head into my room and offered a large clear plastic bag full to the brim with his drug of choice. "Popcorn?"

Tate knew the drill. "No, thanks, Chief. My mom expects me for dinner tonight, and I don't want to ruin my appetite." He glanced up at my dad, who had a strange expression on his face.

"Hey, Dad? You okay?"

"Yep," Dad said quickly. Too quickly.

"Okay. Um, I'm going to hang out with Tate on Sunday. That alright?"

I was eighteen, and I didn't have to ask, but I also didn't want to be rude to my parents. I'd also downgraded our date to a hangout, and I could see from Tate's frown that he noticed.

Change was slow and hard sometimes. I was easing into Tate being something more than my buddy, because if this was real—as I wanted it to be—I wanted to make sure it lasted.

Plus, I didn't know if my overly protective dad would be willing to let Tate hang out as much if he knew we were kissing.

Correction. If he knew we'd had one kiss.

Just one.

"Sure," Dad said easily enough. "Have fun. Let me know where you're going and when you'll be back."

I nodded.

"Popcorn, Audrey?" Dad offered me the bag.

"No, I'm not hungry yet."

"Okay. Pork chops tonight," he said, and I suppressed a whine.

Everyone knew I hated pork chops, but they were his favorite, so several times a month we had them for dinner. Dad stuck a hand in his bag o' popcorn and kept going down the hall.

I glanced at Tate and giggled, figuring I'd ask Dad what was up after Tate left. Tate stifled a smile, because he knew my dad almost as well as I did. Tim Staunton surely had his quirks. Dad served in the Navy on a submarine and survived on a steady diet of popcorn and sweet tea. Twenty-five years later, his diet remained the same. Only now he worked in a firehouse instead of a submarine, and he was waiting for his years of service to pass before retirement.

Tate and my dad got along, and I knew Tate was amused by my dad's eccentricities. But I wondered if that amusement would change to fear if my dad found out what I wanted to do to Tate. With Tate. All over Tate. And let Tate know his opinion on those activities.

Or would Dad accept that his daughter was growing up?

I flipped to another flashcard. "When did the Cuban Missile Crisis end?

Tate answered, and we went back to studying. With my dad on the prowl, we didn't dare do anything but go through flashcards.

Although my mind lingered on kissing.

When it was time for dinner, Tate got up, gathered his backpack, and stood in my room, uncertain.

This time, I wanted to take control, since he'd broken the ice and kissed me first. I rose up and was about to kiss him fast on the lips. But he held my upper arm away from him. As if on cue, my dad popped up in the hall again.

Kiss blocker.

I scowled. Because there was no way I'd kiss Tate in front of my dad, at least not until I felt more comfortable with that activity with Tate.

"I'm on my way out," Tate said to my dad. Then he smiled at me. "See you Sunday," he whispered, and touched my nose with his fingertip. "I'll text you."

I nodded watching him go, and I'd never felt more expectant or happy.

Really, I should have known the moment Dad announced pork chops on the menu that it meant bad news. Especially pork chops coated in Shake N' Bake, my least favorite dinner. It'd be simpler if he just gave me a pig to gnaw on rather than an insipid inch-thick piece of pale gray meat. That way it would at least be a challenge.

I liked food with flavor. I loved anything Mrs. Lemieux cooked. I hated bland.

But it should've been a sign that nothing good would come of this dinner. I should've been prepared.

I wasn't. It blindsided me.

After Tate left, I distracted myself by reenacting our ever-so-quick kiss from yesterday and forgot to think about my dad's behavior. Soon enough we gathered at the dinner table—Dad, my mom, and me. Dad put a chop on my mom's plate and started to cut it. She'd been shaky and weak lately, so he'd been helping her out more.

"Audrey." My dad had a serious look on his face, and it made my stomach plummet. "We have something to tell you."

I glanced between them and noted the matching tight set of their jaws. Panic set in.

Are they moving me away from Tate?

Did Dad lose his job?

Did someone die?

"What is it?" I asked carefully, unfolding my paper napkin and putting it in my lap.

"Mom and I went to the doctor today, and she got a diagnosis."

My breath caught in my throat. Besides the fatigue, she'd also had problems with her vision and with dizziness. She'd visited several doctors who had been unable to find anything. This new doctor had been recommended by her GP.

"I have Multiple Sclerosis," she said, her quivering hand reaching for her fork.

I knitted my brows together. I'd heard of it, but I didn't know anything about it. "What is that?"

"It's a disease where my immune system eats away at the protective cover of my nerves."

We'd always known my mom was tired, but we just thought

it was because of her job as a nursery school teacher. Those kids were exhausting. She hadn't been back to work since her leave of absence, not feeling well enough to last a whole day. But I wasn't expecting *this*.

"Are you going to be okay?" I found myself asking, having trouble processing her words.

"Yes. It's not fatal," Dad said for her. "Lots of people live for years managing MS."

I let out a breath. "Okay."

"But she'll need more care. And we're going to get her a wheelchair."

"Okay," I repeated, my brain whirring. I needed something to do, something to focus on.

My dad passed me the salad, and I loaded up my plate with things other than pork chops.

I ached to pull out my phone and research.

My mom had always been small and frail, tiny boned like a bird. Her ring didn't even fit on my pinkie finger. And she was precious. I was an only child of an only child of an only child. And she'd been my whole world just like I'd been hers. I didn't want her to have to go through anything like this, even if I didn't really know what it meant.

But she was going to be cured. I didn't have to worry.

Right?

I needed to research.

We all chewed our dinner as silence descended on the table. If I were the type to cry, I probably would've, but I was determined not to, so I didn't. After their news, I had no appetite, but I tried to eat my salad, and I pushed around the pork chop.

"We have something to ask you," my dad continued after a bit, and my mom looked miserable as he said it.

Uh oh.

"Anything," I said. "Anything at all."

"Do you mind going to Merlot Valley Community College next year until I can retire? And then we can talk about sending you to New York? We'll need help with cooking and cleaning. And appointments. I can't take care of her if I'm at the station on shift. And I need to get in the years to qualify for the next tier of retirement."

My heart sunk.

My natural reaction was to nod and agree before they even tried to convince me, because I'd do anything to help my mom, and I wouldn't want Dad to have to do everything by himself. Plus, he had to work still, even if his hours were long shifts punctuated with periods of days off.

But I had to think about this.

Because New York. New York meant Tate.

Tate.

"I know this is a lot to ask," my mom said gently, and her eyes welled up, and dammit, I was going to cry. I needed to head this off.

I swallowed hard and shoved all thoughts aside. "Can I get used to the idea? Before I go changing plans?"

"Sure, honey," Dad said.

"Thanks." And I bit the pork and hid my grimace.

My hands were steady. I glanced over at my mom. My hands were steadier than hers.

I can figure this out.

———

After doing the dishes and cleaning up the kitchen, I hurled myself on my bed, on the brink of tears.

My heartbeat raced, and my mouth got dry.

Did my mom being sick mean I'd lose Tate?

Beating my pillow, I scolded myself. This wasn't about me.

It was about my mom. She deserved my care, and I needed to be there for her. I loved her. I'd care for her the best that I could.

In a heartbeat.

But it wasn't that simple.

I writhed on the sheets, running all possibilities through my brain to try to come up with a solution. Wishing everything were different. If we'd caught the MS before, then none of this would have happened. If Dad had started working a year earlier. If I were a better person.

But I couldn't bargain my way out of this.

I curled up in the fetal position and let out a sob.

I thought of Tate. Perfect Tate, who wanted to date me. Tate, with his pouty lips and generous personality and muscles and kindness.

Tate, who filled my heart with joy.

If I stayed home to take care of my mom, what would happen to us? I'd waited years for him.

And now?

Was our relationship destined to never get off the ground? Was it a broken-down train in the station, never to leave?

If only I'd told him how I felt instead of waiting for him. If only we'd done this years ago.

But we hadn't.

My chest tightened, and tears welled in my eyes.

Cold dread came over me, because no solution was acceptable.

God, this hurt.

All the plans we made... New York. London. Japan.

Maybe those were just talk. Tate lived in a different stratos-phere than me. He had the ability to go anywhere and do anything. But it wasn't like I could really do the things we wrote down. My dad made enough to live on, and he was off-the-charts frugal, but his money was nothing like Tate's family. And I didn't have any money.

I'd always be George Bailey, dreaming about the round-the-world trip, but never being able to go.

So, maybe this was a cold dose of reality. My life wasn't dreamy or romantic.

It had disappointments.

And my mom mattered more than anything I was feeling. She needed my care. I'd give it to her.

I flopped over and buried my face in my pillow.

My tears flowed.

They're for my mom, I told myself. *Because she's sick.*

No, I thought. *Be honest. They're for me.*

FOUR
DOUCHEBAG ADVICE
TATE

I n truth, while I had no expectation of getting Audrey naked tomorrow—or indeed any time soon—my anxiety about being a fumbling virgin had overtaken the normal functions of my brain, and I needed answers. My internet searches had given me few useful pointers. I was starting to get desperate.

It was in this vulnerable frame of mind while watching the Giants game on TV Friday night I asked my brothers, "Hypothetically, if I were to get laid, what moves do you recommend?"

Major tactical mistake.

About a year ago, I'd gone to a comedy club with my family, and the comedian chose my dad as his victim/target. Throughout the entire evening, the comedian would turn to my dad and make a comment like, "Isn't that right, Al?" or "I bet your wife likes that, Al." My good-natured dad had taken the ribbing in stride. I'd spent the entire evening grateful the comedian had skipped over me. Growing up with two older brothers, I didn't need to voluntarily be the butt of a joke.

Because I could be one anytime they wanted.

Like now.

Both of them gaped at me as if they couldn't believe I'd asked the question.

Then Perry, my middle brother, responded first, adopting a faux-professorial air. "The most important technique you need to know is how to properly lick her asshole."

At those words, my eldest brother Bert laughed hard, and even I couldn't help my snort. I set down my root beer, closed my eyes, and thought about faking my own death so I'd never have to face Perry or Bert or anyone else again.

Asking these jackasses was such a bad idea.

Perry lounged in Dad's leather wingback chair in the den, pokerfaced, like the jerk hadn't said anything crass, and sipped his ginger ale. Which he drank on the rocks in a crystal old-fashioned glass as if it were whiskey. While wearing striped, tailored pajamas and velvet house slippers. And a top hat. All he needed was an ascot and a pipe to be Hugh Hefner at the Playboy Mansion.

Perry. He was twenty, not seventy-five. He could be hilariously pretentious. *Note to self: get him a smoking jacket for his birthday. Or a monocle.*

After I wrung his neck.

But I was the one dumb enough to ask the question, and I'd expected the useless answer. I'd just hoped I'd get something more.

I sighed and shook my head, exasperated already. "Fuck off. I don't believe you."

"It's how to ease a girl into losing her virginity," Perry insisted, with a smirk he couldn't hide despite trying.

"By rimming," I said flatly. "You're telling me to engage in *rimming* as a beginner's sexual activity. Correction. You are recommending the first sexual act I do with the only girl I've ever liked"—*loved*—"is to apply my tongue to her ass." I threw up my hands. "You're *such* an unromantic bastard. I've never even put my tongue in her *mouth*."

Perry lost the battle with his smirk and his laugh erupted out, evolving into a choked cough. He set his glass down, now in hysterics.

I glared at him. "Dick," I muttered.

All of us swiveled our heads to the television because the centerfielder was up at bat. When he struck out, we collectively groaned. The TV cut to a commercial.

I turned to Bert, who wore gray sweats and a T-shirt like me, rather than fucking silk pajamas like Perry. My oldest brother tended to be more serious than Perry, and I found myself pleading with him, to my embarrassment. In for a penny, though. "Please don't be a douchebag, B. Please tell me the truth."

Bert kicked up his feet on the coffee table and sipped his own soda. At twenty-two, he was the only one old enough to legally drink alcohol, but Mom and Dad had never cared if we drank as long as we didn't leave the house. They said it was safer. And they usually took pictures of our hangovers. Amazingly, they also said they didn't care if we smoked pot, since it was legal. As a result, none of us drank much alcohol or were potheads, likely because our parents were permissive. Reverse psychology worked wonders. Soda for all of us brothers tonight.

Bert looked like he was struggling with whether to answer me seriously or not, and finally ended up shrugging. "Well, rimming is one thing you *can* do as a first sexual activity, although I wouldn't recommend it on the first date. Maybe for Perry, yes. But for you? No."

"Thanks," I said flatly. "You're extremely helpful. What else shouldn't I do? Do I need to bribe you with Warriors tickets to get an answer?"

He shook his head. "Nah. This advice is free. I'm amazed

you're still a virgin. I thought you popped your cherry years ago—"

"Not helping—"

"And I personally think your first sexual activity should be to eat her out."

"Fuck you both," I said with no heat, although my cheeks burned. "I'm sitting here trying to ask you both a serious question, and you're making fun of me. I can learn more from porn than you dumbfucks."

"I'm being honest about going down on her," Bert said, and he gave Perry a "help me out here, bro" look. "It's hot, and it works."

"What do you mean, 'works'?" I asked.

"It'll get her off. She'll come. That's what you want, right?"

I nodded.

"Then that's what you should do. Apply your tongue to her pussy."

"I shouldn't have asked," I groaned, scrubbing my face with my palms.

"I'm serious," Bert insisted. "It's a good first move. I mean, after you get to second base or whatever."

I hadn't gotten to second base. I also didn't want to admit this. "I give up. You guys are no help."

Perry chuckled, picked up his glass, and held up his hands. "Okay, okay. For real, what do you want to know?"

I thought about it. "What was your first time like?"

I knew when both of them got laid, because they told me, but I'd never asked for details. Because eww, brothers. Desperate times, though.

Perry was more promiscuous and more forthcoming than Bert, so his ready response didn't surprise me. "I got off. She didn't. It wasn't my best."

"See?" I said with vehemence, almost knocking over my root

beer. "I want to avoid that. I want to be good at it. The sex thing."

"Most people don't have great sex their first time." He lifted one shoulder in a shrug and drained his drink, his eyes focusing on the opposing team's batter.

"I'm not most people," I said strongly, and I meant it. "I want to make it exceptional for her."

The tone of my voice made both of them stare at me, and I could see their attitudes shifting from making fun of me to helping me out.

And for this, I knew I'd asked the right people. Because while they were my brothers and it was their job to tease me, underneath it all they had my back and would tell me the truth.

Bert studied me. "She matters to you, doesn't she?" His voice had turned quiet and sympathetic, the kindly older brother, the one with a steady girlfriend. The one I needed.

I nodded without hesitation. "Yeah." My voice cracked.

The batter made a base hit, and we all vocalized our protests at the TV.

While the coaches huddled with the pitcher, Bert turned to me, and his voice stayed low and sincere.

"I don't know. There really isn't a specific technique you need to know. There's no magic move. She doesn't have an on button or an off button—although you should be able to find her clit. Honestly, this is what works for me." He leaned forward. "The thing that matters is listening to her, especially to the things she doesn't say. Pay attention. Look at the way she moves and how her body reacts. Repeat the things she likes and keep doing them until she pushes you away. The best advice I can give you is to listen to her body. Oh, and don't do things *to* her. Do things *with* her."

He sat back and sipped his drink, his eyes on the game.

Perry and I took a look at each other and then gaped at Bert.

Noticing us staring at him, Bert asked, "What?"

"That was poetic," Perry whispered in awe.

"Fuck off." Bert's tone was mild, but he hid a smile. "Perry, you'd say that's the truth, isn't it?"

Perry nodded. "You just said it better than I ever could." He turned to me. "When she gets off, she's wet. When she's wet, it feels cherry. When it feels cherry, it's good for both of you."

Bert's lips twitched. "You're a poet in your own way, you know."

A corner of Perry's mouth quirked up in response. "Don't underestimate the middle brother."

"We wouldn't dare," I said. Bert nodded in agreement.

"Tate, I think the problem with you is you're too hesitant," Perry said. "You always want to plan everything and have it be perfect. Sometimes you just have to go in and say *fuck it, I want you*. And go for it, bro. Don't be timid. You're not the kind of guy who'd hurt her. You're plenty confident in all other areas. Just show it."

"Asshole," I muttered. Then, "Thanks."

"You're welcome," they both said at once, and we went back to watching the baseball game.

But I had to ask. "So if I did want to rim her, what the hell would I do?"

They erupted into laughter.

––––––

Later on, after ordering Perry his monocle and smoking jacket, I Googled healthy sex sites, managing to find a few that seemed a bit more than just "wear a condom" and "get tested." My phone buzzed, and I picked it up, thinking it could be Audrey.

But no.

Jade: Want to come to Kevin's party this Saturday? His parents are out of town

Tate: Sorry, no

I felt like an ass for not saying more. But I didn't want to go with her, and I didn't want to go to the party. I never needed to cut loose, because my parents let me do that here.

Still, I felt like my text was too terse.

Tate: I have to work a party for my mom

Jade: And after? It's not a party unless you're there :)

Tate: Probably with Audrey, if I go anywhere

Jade: Oh. Okay

I should just block her number, but Jade hadn't done anything except asked me to a party that probably half the school was going to.

I blinked.

That meant she'd asked me out. I wasn't going to do that to Audrey, who was already sick of how many times Jade texted me.

I blocked Jade's number and deleted the messages. I'd let nothing stand in the way of being with the girl I really wanted.

FIVE

NOT FEELING SORRY

"What do I do now?" I asked, glancing around at the Happy Bear Diner. The diner's decor was a mix of 1950s music, old Mustard Festival posters, carved bear figurines, and pictures of Thai royalty. It also served as my second home, given the amount of time I'd spent here.

I was spending Saturday afternoon here with Wren because after flopping around restlessly all last night, I needed to download everything that had happened with my parents and with Tate and I needed more than texting. I also wasn't telling her in private, because I wasn't going to cry. No crying. Ever. (Again.) So, I wanted a public space.

Plus, the food was good.

I pulled a fry from the plate, dredged it in ketchup, and popped it in my mouth. "I don't know how to make her better. I don't know that there's anything I can do except take her to appointments when my dad is working and help out at home. Apparently, it's going to be hard for her to hold silverware soon, and we have to buy her these special, big plastic kind. My dad's going to put in all sorts of other modifications to the house. She's going to be in a wheelchair. I feel like an idiot that I hadn't realized how much she'd declined over the past few years. It snuck up on me. Now I can see it though, you know?"

"I'm so sorry," Wren whispered, her face falling. She tucked a lock of her straight, dark hair behind her shoulder. "When my dad had his heart attack, it was sudden, and we couldn't plan. We just had to deal with the aftermath. It's amazing how much life can change in a day."

"Or two." I bit into another fry.

Wren's mom owned this diner, which served a combination of classic American food and a secret Thai menu that you had to ask for. I ordered pad Thai and French fries because I could. Wren nibbled on her fresh rolls. Mrs. Namuang never let me pay, although I always tried. She said I'm family. As I grew older, that meant more and more to me.

"Can I whine?"

"Sure," Wren said easily.

"Like, at the Universe? Because I'm pissed at it."

She nodded.

"My mom doesn't deserve to be sick. She's the kindest person. If she were a villain, it would make sense, but she's done nothing wrong."

Wren nodded again but let me talk.

I continued, my words exploding out like a Calistoga geyser. "It sucks that being sick has nothing to do with deserving it. The people who least deserve it get ill, while jerks stay totally healthy. If this world were fair, only assholes would get diseases, while good people would thrive. But it doesn't matter how nice a person you are." I angrily jabbed at the ketchup with another fry. "You can still get really sick. Hence, the Universe sucks."

"I'm sorry," Wren said simply. "It's not fair. How is she taking it?"

"She's frail and shaky. And I'm scared for her."

"Lots of people live with MS for years and years."

I nodded, but I didn't really know that. I didn't know what stage she was in, and I didn't know if my parents were keeping anything else from me. "There's more. My parents asked me to defer entering college and go to community college here."

Wren dropped her fresh roll on her plate, a look of horror on her face. "They asked you to not go to New York?"

"Yep."

"That's ... that's ... *terrible*. All your plans. Are you going to do it? What are you going to do?"

I shrugged and glanced around at the diner. Then I started sketching a design for an outfit on a paper napkin, something I frequently did when I needed to sort out my brain. "I haven't decided yet. They want me to stay here. I think I have to."

Her face fell for the second time in minutes. "But—"

Holding up my hand, I put it to her mouth. "Shh."

"But Audrey," she got out around my palm.

I narrowed my eyes at her. "I'm not going there. I'm not doing it. I'm not thinking it or saying it."

"Fine," she hissed. "I'll go there for you because I'm thinking and saying it. Honey, I feel sorry for you. I know you. You just started dating Tate for real. He finally asked you out. And you want to get the hell out of here. With him. To see the world."

My eyes welled up with tears, and I willed them to stop. "I do," I whispered. "I'm scared of never getting out of here. I'm scared of not being with him."

"Hmm," Wren said. "This major league sucks. Because I'm going to miss you."

I hadn't let myself think about it, but Wren had enrolled at NYU and planned on studying film, with a fervent desire to direct female-centered superhero movies. Add hanging with Wren to the list of things I wasn't going to experience next year.

"I'm going to miss you too. And him. I can't learn fashion design at Merlot Community College. I can't visit all the Ivy

Leagues for inspiration from old buildings and libraries. I'm scared that if I stay here, all my best days will be in high school. Like a total loser."

Wren's face twisted in concern. "Maybe there's a solution." She sipped her Thai iced tea then reached over and tapped my hand. "Putting off a dream doesn't mean it won't ever happen. You can still have all the things you want. It'll just take a bit longer."

That really made me want to cry. "Tate wrote up a list of things that he and I were going to do."

"Oh? What kind of list? Did it have naughty things on it?"

A gleam shone in her eye, and I shoved her hand away. "Not *that* kind of list," I insisted, although my skin zinged with the thought. "Tate made up a list of places to visit, and the way he talked about it, it felt like we could really go. I just have never traveled. Unlike everyone else. You go places."

"We travel to Thailand about every year or so."

"See? We don't. My dad plans a family trip for us every other year to visit his parents in Mississippi."

"What did Tate say when you told him about your mom?"

"I haven't told him yet."

She blinked.

I held up my hand. "Yes, we can talk about that, but one issue at a time. What am I going to do if I'm at home and everyone else is gone and doing their thing?"

"You could work. Have you thought about getting a job?"

No, I hadn't thought about that. I was still in shock from my mom's news. "You're right. I probably should. It has to be something that won't interfere with my mom's doctor's appointments and therapy."

She clapped her hands. "I know! You should go work on the train! That's just evenings and weekends."

"The wine train?" I asked incredulously. The famous

Napa Valley Wine Train served a very fancy dinner (and sometimes lunch) along the rails in the neighboring valley. But that train literally didn't go anywhere. It took hours to crawl up the valley and then back again. Talk about a train to nowhere.

"Think about it. It's good money. They hire eighteen-year-olds, too."

It wasn't the worst idea I'd ever heard. If I had to stay, maybe I could work on the train. Then it would seem like I was going places. "I'll look into it," I said. I picked up the ketchup to add more, and it spurted all over my hands. "Guh, let me clean this off."

I stood up and went to the bathroom. When I inspected myself in the mirror, I noticed my brown eyes had become glossy, and I had dark circles under them from not sleeping last night.

It's gonna be okay, girl.

I sighed.

I wished my life were different.

And somehow, looking at myself in the mirror, I knew I needed to stop wishing for that, because it wasn't going to happen. I needed to play with the cards I'd been dealt.

I could do this. I could take care of my mom and wait on my dream. Even though it felt like my world was crashing down now, in a few years I'd look back and realize it was all for the best.

After washing my hands and checking my face, I returned and slid into the booth across from Wren, who had unapologetically stolen one of my fries.

"Now can we talk about Tate?"

"Sure."

Wren's tone was gentle. "What's going to happen when school starts in the fall?"

"If I take care of my mom, he goes away. I don't." My lip trembled.

"That can't be the answer, though. You just got him for real. You can't let him leave. Not while you're just starting something. You need to do some sort of big gesture. Show him how you feel with large notecards."

"You've watched *Love, Actually* too many times, and I don't even know if I have him for real. I have him for now."

"God," she hissed. "This is depressing! And come fall, Jade heads to the East Coast, too, right? At Penn?"

I will not cry.

"Don't remind me. It's not the end of the world," I said reasonably, feeling like it was the end of the world.

"It's huge! You're sacrificing your future."

I narrowed my eyes at her. "Every noble and wonderful thing in this world is based on sacrifice." I threw up my hands. "I don't want to call what I'm doing a sacrifice. I'm not sacrificing a damned thing. I'm getting my mom. My family. It's an opportunity for me to show how much I care."

"If you give up your new boyfriend and your college experience, you're going to resent it."

"Would you give those up for your mom?" I challenged. "In my place, what would you do?"

She studied me. "Okay, yeah. I'd take care of my mom."

"See? I'm making the same choice you would."

"But what about Tate?"

I let out a sigh. "I don't know," I whispered. "It feels like we just started, only to stop. We've done nothing. And I have all these feelings for him. I've barely kissed him, and I want to do more."

"Would you sleep with him?" she asked.

A warm feeling expanded in my chest. "I would. I want to do everything with him. Every. Thing. I'd let—"

"Are you going to talk about that with him?"

"Sleeping with him?" I squeak.

"Yes, but I was talking about staying here. If you decide to do that."

"I'm scared," I admit. "This is new and fragile. He just admitted he liked me. But yes, I'll talk with him."

"Good. You guys are meant for each other." Her face dropped. "But it'll just hurt more when he leaves, huh?"

"Yeah," I said. I ate a fry. "Is it bad that I want to have this summer with him? Even if I have to let him go at the end?"

"Why don't you let him decide?"

"We can decide it together. It's too early to ask him now. I'll see how it goes."

She nodded.

"Are you going to hold back with him knowing that he's leaving? I mean emotionally as well as physically."

"I don't want to. While everything in me is screaming to protect my heart, I want him. In all the ways." I caught her eyes. "Does that make me a bad person?"

"To want to sleep with a hot guy you've liked for years? No. But to get all cozy with him and then send him to the other side of the country? That's a recipe to hurt both of you. Listen, I fully support you taking care of your mom and getting closer with the one guy you have wrapped around your finger. But I will not support you dumping him at the end of summer."

My voice lowers. "I don't want to do that."

But was that something that would happen?

"There isn't an easy answer," she said. "But you're going on a date with him tomorrow?"

I nodded.

"And you're going to eventually talk with him?"

I nodded again.

She smiled. "Then let me come over and help you pick out an outfit."

"Thanks," I said.

We left to go to my house while I secretly obsessed over what I'd do without Tate in my life.

SIX

EMOJIS

After spending all day Saturday working with my mom catering a wedding at a local boutique hotel, I crawled into the MLR and grabbed my phone. It was late at night. I'd been so busy serving hors d'oeuvres I hadn't been able to text Audrey, even though I'd thought about her every time I passed the cake. Not only was it sweet like her, but I kinda wished the topper looked like us. And was at our wedding.

Audrey was accustomed to me having these jobs on weekends, especially in summer. Years ago, Mom decided Perry, Bert, and I needed to know how to serve food and act at parties. Today, I'd failed in both those endeavors since I caused a minor food-related disaster that didn't make Mom happy. I sighed.

Safe in the cab of my truck and eager to contact Audrey now that I was free, I had half a mind to drive over to her house despite the hour. Instead, my fingers dashed over the phone screen.

Tate: Guess how many mini lobster rolls wrapped in tiny red and white checked paper bags I dropped?

Audrey: More than one?

Tate: Two trays. On the prep kitchen floor. Made such a huge mess. Mom was pissed

Tate: I'm no model employee

Tate: I might be out of a job for a while

Tate: Like at least until next weekend when she has another big bash

Tate: More time to hang with you, though. :)

Audrey: Sorry about the event, but to be fair, I'm sorrier about the loss of the lobster rolls. Your mom's are yummy

Tate: You wound me

Audrey: Kidding. I'm sorry about your job loss

Tate: So

Tate: About that date. Still wanna go on one with a hapless waiter?

Audrey: Absolutely <3

Tate: Pick you up tomorrow at noon. Missed you today. Night. x

I wondered after I hit send whether I should've included the x, but I settled on liking the fact that I sent it. If I couldn't kiss her for real, I'd kiss her virtually.

Audrey: Night. x

I smiled to myself.

The next afternoon, I took my seat in a booth across from Audrey at Craft, a Sonoma classic food institution, thinking about how much between us was the same and how much was, I hoped, about to change.

Despite having eaten here with Audrey dozens of times, today felt different because of what I wanted to ask her.

The host left us menus, and I took in Audrey's beauty.

Dressed in a classic blue-striped sailor shirt, tiny white shorts, and strappy espadrilles, she was my hot girl fantasy.

But some concerning tiredness in her eyes hadn't been present the last time we saw each other. I hung out with her so frequently, I often knew when she was sick or about to get her period, even when she hadn't figured those things out herself. I guess I knew when she was off because she was my everything. But I didn't know what this current down-in-the-dumps expression meant.

"Are you worried about finals?" I asked, furrowing my eyebrows.

Audrey blinked rapidly at me, picked up the menu, then shot me a grin that didn't meet her eyes. "No. Why?"

I opened my mouth to explain, but the waiter sidled up to the table and took our drink order—house-made sodas.

Maybe I should've taken us somewhere where we wouldn't be interrupted. This better not be as bad as the picnic tables at school the other day.

Not wanting to be inadvertently insulting, I needed to choose my words carefully. "You look a little tired."

"Oh." She quieted, and I kicked myself for not saying something nice. It wasn't that she didn't look fantastic, but it seemed like something troubled her. "I didn't sleep well."

I got an image of Audrey all curled up in her bed, her long hair splayed across a snowy white pillow and immediately banished that thought to my spank bank. It didn't belong in my brain now. I'd take it out later when I could do something with it.

"Anything else going on?" I tried to keep my voice quiet.

She peered at me over the menu. I didn't know why she bothered reading the entrees. It wasn't like she ever ordered anything but the truly outstanding grilled cheese anyway.

This fact heartened me.

I *knew* her. I loved the fact that I knew her possibly better than she knew herself, the advantage of years of studying her. Hopefully I wasn't too stalkery. I just cared.

Audrey didn't answer me for a beat. Then another. "Family stuff," she finally said. "My mom is sick."

"What kind of sick?"

"She's got MS."

My stomach dropped. "Is she going to be okay?"

Audrey nodded. "Yeah, I think so. She should live a long time. But she'll be in a wheelchair soon."

"Babe. I'm so sorry."

"Thanks," she said. "Honestly, I don't want to talk about it now. We can talk about it later. Okay?"

I nod. "If that's what you want. You know you can talk about anything with me, right?"

"Yeah. I know."

This was a huge setback, but I decided not to push her, especially when she didn't want to talk about it. We'd have plenty of time later. I'd help her process it.

"Distract me, okay?" she whispered. "Tell me something."

I paused, thinking. "Perry got a Vespa. He has this set of goggles that makes him look steampunk. I swear my brother cosplays his real life."

She laughed. "What color is the scooter?"

"Black. I have no idea how he plans to pick up a date on that thing."

"Maybe she'll just have to have her own. They can ride together."

I smiled. "I can see that."

Our beverages got delivered, and again we were left alone. I glanced up at her as she sipped her drink, her cute nose scrunching at the bubbles.

She said to distract her.

I had a huge distraction.

I *wanted* this girl sitting across from me.

Bert had been right. I needed confidence, and the glacial pace I'd set needed to speed up.

The time had come to make my move.

If I asked her and she said no, I might fuck up our friendship for the rest of our lives, and I wasn't sure my heart could take that. In fact, I knew it couldn't.

But if I didn't ask her, my heart would hurt worse. It would split or possibly dissolve.

I couldn't stand it anymore. I *had* to ask. I *had* to take the next step.

So here I was, putting myself on the line, with no other choice.

Now or never.

My heart started racing, and my palms got clammy. "Can I ask you something?"

"Sure." Her cautious tone meant she knew this wouldn't be a normal conversation. A variety of emotions flittered across her face—apprehension, excitement, confusion.

I leaned forward and lowered my voice. *Stay calm. Start simple.* "Would it freak you out if I told you I like you? That I like you very much?" My heart pounded in my ears, and my stomach clenched, waiting for her to respond.

Audrey closed her eyes and blushed. "No. I like you, too." A delicate finger reached out and hooked my index finger, then she let it go and glanced away, like she'd assumed too much.

She got it wrong. Her easy tone told me she thought I meant I liked her as friends.

I didn't.

This wasn't going the way I hoped, and I needed to say it better. I leaned in closer, and she finally looked at me with both trust and wariness in her brown eyes.

"No, that's not what I meant. What I want to know is, would it freak you out if you knew that I like you as more than friends." I scrubbed my hands over my cheeks. "That I want to date you. More than only today. I mean, I'm asking you if you want to be my girlfriend, not just my friend. Because I really, really like you. A lot."

God, I was a fool, but at least the words had left my mouth, and I hadn't died yet, nor had she slapped me or run away. So those were two things on my side.

I waited for her response, as the rise and fall of the sun hung in suspense.

"You do?" The innocent surprise on her face hurt my solar plexus.

Has she not known how much I adore her? God, I'm an asshole.

"Yeah." My voice came out husky. "I've been waiting for you to decide if I was what you wanted, because I knew that you were all I wanted. But I can't wait anymore. I have to know. Will you be my girlfriend?"

Now she nodded repeatedly, and her cuteness made my heart thump more. How could she doubt how much I wanted her? "Yes. I agree. I'd love to. Date, I mean. Be my boyfriend. I mean, your girlfriend. I mean," she sighed, frustration clear as she stumbled on the words too. "I'd like us to be boyfriend-girlfriend. I like you a lot. Also." The fact that she fumbled over her words made me happy in a weird way, because it wasn't just me. Despite our easy conversation on everything else, neither one of us was good at talking about what we meant to each other.

Still, the binds around my heart eased up, and my heart rate calmed down. But then what we'd just finished saying dawned on me and my pulse jacked right up again.

I had a girlfriend, the only girlfriend I'd ever craved. *Audrey was mine.*

Yes.

I restrained myself from bounding across the table to kiss her, since I should just let her drink her root beer in peace. Still, I practically pulsed, wanting to run around the restaurant to burn off energy.

"I'm glad we waited," she said. "Because I really like you." Her face reddened. "I've liked you this whole time, actually."

Again, my heart soared. "You have?"

"Yeah."

"It's mutual." I grinned like crazy now. "Completely."

Now that my secret was out in the open, a weight lifted from my shoulders. The knowledge that I liked her was a heavy book I'd put in my backpack no one could see. Now that I'd taken it out, I didn't miss it. I only noticed how good I felt not having to carry it around with me.

Everything was right in the world, and she could be mine. Forever.

The waiter came back, and we ordered. I almost told him she'd want the grilled cheese, but I didn't want to be that arrogant prick who didn't let his girlfriend talk. I just liked taking care of her and learning every single thing about her. There was so much to know and adore.

Also. *Girlfriend.*

When he left, and after Audrey ordered the grilled cheese, I took both of her hands in mine and asked, "Where do you want to go after lunch? Do you need to go back home?"

A fleeting, far-away look passed behind her eyes.

"Do you need to go spend time with your mom?"

She straightened and brightened. "No, I don't have to go home right now. My dad is with her. Where do you want to go?"

"We could go to Black Bishop Winery to see the art, if you like."

Audrey's face took on that contented look she always got

when I suggested something that surprised and pleased her. Like I'd granted a wish she didn't know she had. "Sounds like fun. I haven't been there in years." Then she tilted her head to the side. "Do you think I'll ever like wine?"

I chuckled. "No. Never. Not my Audrey."

My Audrey.

You couldn't escape wine in Merlot. Vineyards and wineries were interwoven into our town's history and a huge source of business and tourism. Our school mascot was the Grape Crushers. Many homeowners even had rows of grapes in their backyards.

So, the fact that Audrey hated wine really stuck out, especially since tourists couldn't get enough of the stuff. While her parents weren't as permissive as mine, they, like mine, didn't care if she had a sip every once in a while. But there was no chance of her turning into a wino.

That didn't mean she wouldn't enjoy Black Bishop, though.

Tasting rooms in Napa and Sonoma Counties varied widely. Some massive estates loomed large in the landscape, with space to picnic among tasteful gardens. Other locations were nestled behind unmarked gates so secretive, you basically had to be my mom to get a tasting. And still others offered attractions besides the wines, which was helpful when you were, oh, eighteen, and couldn't legally try said beverages.

But even among all the wineries, Black Bishop stood out.

Besides the galleries, the small, private grounds had an excellent backdrop—a view of the valley. A fantastic place to turn our second kiss into an *event*.

Our food came soon enough, and we dug in, chatting about finals and graduation.

After we ate lunch, I paid, despite her protest and attempt to pay for half. "I asked you out, and this is our first date. You can take me out sometime, but this was my treat," I said firmly.

Audrey paused for a moment to consider, then her smile hit me in the feels. "I will. Thank you." She took my hand as we left, and it felt right. We should've been doing that long ago.

We stepped outside into the warm, clear afternoon. Since I wanted to catch the sunset, we needed to take our time getting up to Black Bishop. So, I had another errand to do with her.

In my truck, Audrey went to put on her seatbelt in her usual space, but she was too far away. I knew it was cheesy to have her sit right beside me in a pickup truck. Buuuttt—

Fuck it. "Scoot so you're beside me," I said.

She gave me a sideways glance. "Are you ordering me around?"

Yes? No? "Maybe?"

"Okay." And easy as that, she slid over and belted herself in next to me. I wrapped an arm around her and smiled into her shoulder, then started the MLR. She smelled like strawberries.

I drove until we turned into the parking lot of Walgreens.

A suspicious expression came over Audrey's face. "You're not buying condoms, are you?" Then her cheeks reddened, and her hand flew to her mouth. "Oh, god. I said that out loud. Shoot me."

A laugh burst out of me. "No," I stuttered. "Nothing like that. Trust me." I climbed out of the car and pulled her with me, trying not to think of condoms.

Which I'd already bought.

Instead, we went to the photo counter, staffed by Hunter, a junior I knew from football. He gave us a halfhearted smile, clearly sick of working at this place and dealing with the public. "Can I help you?" he asked morosely.

"We need to take passport photos," I said. "Or actually, Audrey does."

She turned to me, her lips parting in surprise. "Passport photos? You *can't* surprise me with those. Before I take photos that are going to last for ten years, I need to do my hair! And I don't have lip gloss—"

"You look beautiful," I assured her, giving her fingers a squeeze. "And if you don't like them, we'll retake them until you do."

The smile that spread across her face made my heart soar. "God, you really are the best." It looked like she was going to lean up and kiss me, and I held my breath. But instead, she stepped over to the wall, stood in front of the white background, and smiled for Hunter as he fumbled with the camera. He took a few pictures, and when he nodded that he got the shot, he let her review them. She approved, and he printed a set for her.

"One step closer to the Anti-Bucket List," I murmured as I paid for them, again over her protest. "I made you an appointment to get your passport, too."

She shook her head silently at me, a strange wistful expression on her face, and held my hand as we returned to the truck. "You're incredible, Tate."

Back in the MLR, we headed up the hills to the stylish concrete posts signaling the winery entrance and pulled into a gravel parking lot. I stopped and helped her out of the car, proud she was by my side.

We walked up to the glass and concrete building hand in hand, chewing on spearmint gum from Walgreens. Fresh breath mattered. Even more now that we might kiss.

Sidestepping Black Bishop's tasting room, which had a line out the door, we walked inside the main building and stopped short. An involuntary chuckle came out of me.

In the gallery, a glass eggplant lay next to a glass peach on a Lucite pedestal, lighted as if the sculptures were Tiffany jewelry.

Audrey snorted, standing stock still. "Is this emoji art? That's a dick and a butt, isn't it?"

I grinned. "Yep. What do you think?"

Whirling around in a slow circle, she took in the scene before us. "I think it's *awesome.*"

Black Bishop winery, run by family friends, was home to the weirdest art collection this side of San Francisco. The funky, rotating collections were the closest thing to an art museum in Merlot.

Audrey and I wandered through the exhibit, hand in hand. The artist had taken emojis and recreated them in blown glass, then arranged them so they said something. It was the viewer's job to figure out what they meant. Some were easy, like a thumb's up or a purple devil's face. But others?

"A cherry and a dog?" Audrey asked.

"Oh my god." I laughed. "Perry texts that all the time, in response to just about anything. 'Cherry, Dawg.'" I shook my head. "He's such a ... a ... *Perry.*" I turned to the next. "Lipstick and a horse?"

"Kiss my ass," she read solemnly from a card to the side. We burst out laughing, and I wrapped my arm around her shoulders.

Slow and steady, moving from hand holding to bodies touching. She bumped into me playfully with her shoulder, and I held her closer.

"Red prohibited sign, clock, bull, poop?" She squinted at the card. "No time for your bullshit."

But as fun as the art was, what mattered was holding Audrey's hand and bumping shoulders with her and having my arm wrapped around her and getting our bodies to touch each other and simply spending time laughing with her, with our boundaries down. With her as my *date*, not just my friend.

An afternoon that for the first time ever had the possibility for *more.*

"Do you want to go outside," I suggested after we'd seen everything. "Check out the gardens?"

I couldn't care less about the gardens. My thoughts were on other things.

"Sure," she agreed easily enough.

We stepped outside into the sunlight and the green vines, and walked along the gravel path, as the light shone on the gilt edges of her auburn hair.

"It's pretty out here," she said, taking in the landscape, her eyes wide.

"So are you," I said, focusing on her.

I turned so we faced each other, all of the valley below us, a patchwork of vineyards and houses and farms. The only person I saw—the only one I'd ever wanted—wasn't even a foot away from me. I peered down at her.

God, she's gorgeous.

My heart pounded, and I felt dizzy. I could do this. I'd planned this. It was going to be perfect.

I stepped in closer and traced her cheek with my finger. Then I dropped my hand to my pocket because my palms had become clammy, and I was barely keeping them from shaking. My dick was definitely paying attention and taking notes on the proceedings.

Audrey's eyes caught mine, at first questioning, then widening with wonder, and then softening with a small nod.

Permission.

She wanted me, too. And unlike in her room, she was ready.

I leaned in, tilting my face towards Audrey for our first real kiss.

A female voice sounded behind me. "Tate Lemieux, is that you? And Audrey Staunton?" Audrey and I both jumped apart, startled.

I turned around to a tiny woman in Birkenstocks and brown

clothes from the 1970s. She held the hand of a bigger woman, with tattoos up and down her arms.

Oh, fuck. It was our ninth grade health teacher and her wife. My entire body screamed in protest.

Figured. I finally got the nerve to tell Audrey how I felt and to kiss her for real and we ran into the woman who taught us about reproduction. Who lectured us for days and days on the parts of the male and female genitalia. A woman who projected a diagram of the male reproductive system on the wall, then hit it with the pointer stick so every guy in the room winced.

I winced at the memory.

Shoot me now.

Audrey looked as embarrassed as I felt. "Hi, Mrs. Sanchez."

"It's very good to see you. Are you looking forward to gradu-ation?" she asked us, a curious expression on her face, like she didn't know she'd just interrupted the most important moment of my life. Like I wasn't about to kiss the only girl I've ever loved, and she ruined it.

Not that I was bitter.

"Yeah, um," I said.

"You have to enjoy the last of these high school days before they're gone." She squeezed the hand of her wife. "But this place is wonderful. Jennie and I like to come here often for the exhibits."

"Us too. Or, that's why we're here."

One of the reasons.

Mrs. Sanchez said, "Plus, we're members of their wine club. You should tell your parents to check it out."

The grin on my face turned manic.

Audrey saved the day. "I'm sure Lemieux Catering has been here plenty."

"True, true." Mrs. Sanchez kept beaming at us.

"Well, it's been nice to see you. Will we be seeing you at graduation?" Audrey asked.

"Absolutely. It's always bittersweet because you are going away to college, but I'm proud of both of you and your accomplishments. Where are you headed?"

I itched to leave, recalibrating my plans, so I blurted out, "Columbia. Audrey's going to the Fashion Institute of Technology in Manhattan. We both got into our first choice schools." Audrey crossed her arms over her chest, her lips pressed tight for some reason. "But right now, I was just going to go show Audrey the view."

"That sounds wonderful. You're going to have the best time. Well, we must be off," Mrs. Sanchez said. "Lovely to see you both."

She turned, and I exhaled, then tugged Audrey with me further down the garden, away from the tasting room and art exhibit and our health teacher and her wife.

"God, that was embarrassing," I muttered.

"No kidding," Audrey agreed, and I squeezed her hand.

Her getting me on a deep level was one of the myriad reasons why I liked her and why nothing was going to change after I kissed her.

We looked at the world the same way.

I could do this.

I swiveled my head around searching for lurking parents, teachers, administrators, coaches, or classmates. "Anyone else going to sneak up on us?"

She chuckled. "I don't think so."

"Good," I said, and crashed my mouth to hers.

SEVEN

GAME CHANGER

O n a normal day when I sucked on my usual blow pop, I put off getting to the center because I loved the anticipation. The waiting. While the bubblegum flavor didn't last long, and it was a lot of work for little reward, each time I'd work for that magical moment when I broke through to the drool-inducing gum.

With bigger events in my life like Christmas or birthdays, I'd almost set myself afire with excitement as the dates got closer and closer and the delicious tension mounted. I'd count down the days on my Cillian Murphy calendar. When the event finally came, I often mused afterwards that the waiting had been so much better than the real thing.

Perhaps I lived too much in my imagination. I often found it hard to stay in the moment and really *enjoy* whatever it was I'd been desperately waiting for.

But I'd been waiting for Tate Lemieux to kiss me like this—a real, passionate kiss, with tongue and feeling—*for years*, and unlike an event on my calendar or the gum in the middle of the blow pop, there'd never been any reasonable certainty it'd happen. I couldn't count on it like my birthday. It was just a dream in the middle of the night, or something to imagine while reading very dirty things in *Cosmo*.

At least I'd had no hope until he'd pecked me on the lips a few days ago. After that, I'd allowed wings to flutter in my chest.

But the experience of receiving a real kiss from Tate? Feeling his soft lips pressed to mine? Overwhelming me? Cradling me?

I *combusted*.

Tate's kiss was exponentially better than I'd ever imagined—and I'd imagined it quite a bit, in vivid detail. Whatever the opposite of disappointed was, I was that. Buzzing, elated, turned on.

Seconds ago, with a gentle groan, Tate had urged my lips apart, his tongue touched mine, and I tasted the spearmint on his breath. I *loved* his taste. I loved the sexy feel of his wet tongue inside my mouth. I adored *everything* about him.

I felt alive.

And I wanted to pinch myself because we were finally kissing.

How did I ever get so lucky?

My body trembled as he held me and while I, well, sucked his face back.

Because he was Tate—the most romantic guy, the consummate planner, the supremely thoughtful person—he'd taken me to the best view in the valley, on the prettiest day of the year, and kissed me passionately in a gorgeous garden after feeding me my favorite lunch and giving me the gift of a day of art.

Oh, and he gave me the gift of *possibility*, by taking me to get passport photos.

It couldn't get any better than this.

Here, right now, was my birthday wish come true.

But as he kissed me, my knees gave way and he held me up

tighter, clutching me while our surroundings swirled about us—
or at least it felt that way.

Tate gave me a *game changer* kiss. One that turned us from
dancing around each other to dancing *with* each other. One that
changed us from being friends to being a couple. A pair.

True boyfriend and girlfriend.

Finally.

My arms wrapped around his neck as I gave him back everything he gave me and more, which was hard to match since he
was damn good at kissing. His hands clutched my waist tight. I
expected him to move them down to my butt and do sexy-
naughty moves from *Cosmo*, but he didn't.

Because he was Tate.

Sweet and hot and sensitive to my needs. Not one to press
to his advantage. The best boy I'd ever known.

But maybe a little *too* sweet.

I wanted him to touch me, squeeze my ass, do *something*, so
I wiggled into him, and he smiled against my mouth, and I loved
that too.

We broke apart for a moment and panted, staring at each
other with matching goofy grins on our faces.

"Wow," I whispered, and I chided myself for not coming up
with something more memorable to say.

"I could kiss you again," he said quietly, and I nodded and
tilted my lips up to meet his.

Then our mouths found each other once more, this time
more careful and exploratory. He smelled like Tate, the tall,
handsome boy he was, and tasted minty fresh, and his *presence*
assaulted my senses—his body was so alive, and his warmth
enveloped me. And I didn't think I'd ever stop kissing him. I'd
never want to.

Forget *Cosmo's* tips. Tate knew what he was doing, which

surprised me. I thought he didn't have much experience. Maybe he was a natural.

But the kiss turned into a bruising ache for me because at this moment, even if I hadn't said anything to my parents about their request, I had to stay home. And this boy who I've wanted to kiss forever wasn't gonna be mine forever, because the right thing to do was to let him go to college without me. I couldn't hold him back from his dreams.

So, a decision must be made.

Did I stop this?

Or did I do everything we could do before he left?

That was a no-brainer. I couldn't help myself.

I wanted him. All of him.

And my body wanted him, too. I'd touch any part of him and let him touch any part of mine. Full stop, I wanted to be a virgin no more. And I wanted him to be the one to change that for me.

Because doing it with anyone else wasn't acceptable. How could it be, when all I ever wanted—*who* I ever wanted—stood right here with me, holding me, kissing me?

I didn't know how I'd eventually give him up, but I'd have to do it. And that made me more and more desperate for his touch.

We kissed and kissed and kissed, and when he pressed closer, I felt a stiffness against my belly, which took me a moment to realize what it was.

He had an erection, and that gave me a whole other set of tingly emotions and desires. I *loved* it. It was the first time I'd ever been close to a guy's hard dick—one I lusted after. I wanted to see it. I wanted to know more about it.

"I think we need to go," I whispered when I was so wound up I couldn't take it anymore. The sun inched lower on the horizon. If we stayed put, we'd be arrested for public indecency at the rate my brain was going. "At least we can't stay here. But I don't want to leave."

"Me neither. Wanna go home?"

I nodded, then came to my senses and shook my head. "Can we just get in your truck?" And I licked my lips.

His dark blue eyes went comically wide, and he grabbed my hand. "C'mon." Then we walked so fast I laughed.

He dragged me to the driver's side and opened that door first, which was the first time he'd ever done that. "Here," he said. For a moment, I questioned his actions, not because I was some sort of princess who needed him to open the passenger side, but because he confused me.

Then I figured out what he wanted, and I was *so* on board. "Okay," I whispered.

I climbed up the seat, and he followed me into the Mobile Living Room. After he placed his butt behind the wheel, he closed the door. I kneeled next to him and leaned into his body, and conversation ceased.

Immediately, Tate's mouth seared mine, kissing me with a hunger that took my breath away. He started to press me backward into the passenger side of the bench seat, my legs splaying on either side of his waist so he was almost on top of me, until I pushed him back on his shoulders. He went upright in his seat rather willingly, although there *was* a grumble of protest in the back of his throat that did things to me.

I loved the grumble, and I loved that he did what I asked.

I loved that he wanted me and that I could trust him.

I loved that I could have him now. While we'd been orbiting around each other for years, and I didn't want to look desperate, I still wanted madly to throw myself at him.

When else was I going to get the chance?

So, here goes nothing.

With one hand on each of his shoulders, I crawled into his

lap to straddle him, and my ass made the horn honk. "Oh, shit," he cursed. We both ducked instinctively, then giggled into each other, collapsing into each other's arms with laughter.

Our noses brushed together, and we giggled, holding each other.

I loved that we could laugh together, even now. Even while exploring being together as more than friends. Even when we were both nervous and out of our leagues. Even though this was new.

Because we could support each other. Because we were made for each other. Because he was, quite simply, mine.

I straddled him as we kissed. He made a low noise in the back of his throat because now we had some friction between us. His hard boy parts filled the space against my damp girl parts, and you bet I liked the way it felt. My shorts weren't thick, and I could feel his bulge, and it felt better than anything *Cosmo* ever told me.

Dry humping for the win.

"If you keep rubbing like that, I'm going to come in my pants," he warned.

"Sorry." I stiffened my shoulders and pulled back. "I don't. I haven't—"

He cut me off. "It's new for me too. Don't worry." His hand held my lower back toward him, and his voice was sexy deep. "And it's fine, but I wanted you to know what you're doing to me. Also, the zipper hurts," he admitted, adjusting himself beneath me.

"Sorry," I said again.

"Don't be." He sighed, having moved his dick. "That's better."

I reached a tentative hand down and stroked him through his jeans, and he grunted so loudly I thought I did something wrong.

"Audrey," he said, his tone reverent, his hands framing my face. "You're beautiful. You really are my everything."

This guy. "I am?"

He nodded. "You have been for a long time."

"It's been that way for me too," I acknowledged, and felt the soft skin under his T-shirt where I held him at his waist. I was dying to see him up close with his shirt off, because I knew from pool parties that it would be delectable. *Very* delectable.

Tate kissed me a bit rougher than before, and I gave it back to him just the same, free from the friend-zone restrictions we had before. But still it wasn't enough. I had to explore him, and I needed him to do the same to me. As far as I could tell, he wanted the same thing.

He tugged on a tendril of my hair. "I love your hair." He gestured down my body. "And fuck. You're so hot."

"You can touch me," I whispered, "I mean you can touch my body. *Anywhere.* I want you to." And he smiled like I gave him the best present ever. The look of wonder on his face made my heart soar.

"I want to," he said. "But I don't want to push you or hurt you—"

I shut him up with a kiss, grabbed one of his big hands, and cupped it over my clothes on my breast.

The tortured, hot noise he made drew a similar one out of me.

He squeezed gently, taking his time, but again, I didn't want him to. So I took matters into my own hands, so to speak. I fell backward into the front seat, drawing him with me, and pulled up my striped sailor shirt past my chest so he could see my white lacy bra underneath. It was of the see-through variety. The kind where they airbrushed out the nipples on advertising images. In other words, it wasn't a prudish bra.

Tate seemed to like it, based on his whispered, *"Fuck."* He bent down and placed a kiss between my breasts. "I can't believe we're doing this," he said in awe. "After all this time." Kissed above my breast. "I've wanted you so damn much."

Before I could do it, he tugged down the cup of my bra and sucked my nipple into his mouth, his warm tongue caressing me. I gasped at the touch, because I was super sensitive there.

"When I, um, take care of myself, I always play with my nipples." I blurted out somewhat stupidly, but it wasn't like we had any more secrets between each other.

Well, maybe we had one. But I'd talk to him about that. Later. Now was not the time.

He groaned loudly and lunged up to kiss me, his hand kneading my boob in a way I discovered I really liked—rough and tender at the same time.

"I only think of you," he said, and that admission made me even more aroused. He kissed me again, with so much heat, and his hand started to make its way to the waist of my shorts.

But then we heard tires crunch on the gravel and remembered that we were in public in daylight. Anyone could catch us.

He quickly rearranged my shirt and bra and pulled me up. He tried to smooth my clothes out, but he couldn't do that great of a job, so I took over. Still, we managed to get both of us put back together.

Although, to be fair, he looked like he'd been making out, and I was surely the same. Since his hair was usually tousled, it took very little for him to get back to normal, but kissing had plumped his lips. And he was still very, very hard. I glanced down at his jeans and raised an eyebrow. "Are you going to be okay?"

"Yeah," he said, his voice strangled. "Well, no, I don't think I'm ever going to be okay after today, but not every erection needs a release."

I laughed and kissed him again, this time sweetly on the cheek. We both sighed, and he put his finger on the ignition. "Where to?"

"I told my parents I'd be home for dinner. You want to join us?"

"No, thanks," he said, almost automatically. "But I'll drive you home."

And we drove home listening to his music and talking like we always did.

Only now, for the first time, we'd broken in the Mobile Living Room. I couldn't wait to see what more we could do on this secret list I was creating in my mind.

———

When I arrived home, kiss-stung and rumpled, I beelined into my room and plopped on the bed. I let out a breath, and my thoughts scattered everywhere like debris from a derailed train.

Our relationship—this one I'd wanted for four years—was just starting, and now I feared it'd be over before it even began.

And I was scared to bring it up with Tate because talking about it wouldn't fix anything.

I faced an impossible decision. If I chose my family and stayed home, I'd be doing what was right. What I *should* do. I'd honor my mom and help my dad. Given what I'd read on MS and the progress of her disease, soon enough she'd need help with basic things like eating, plus I'd need to take her to therapy when Dad was on shift. He could still continue working until he reached his full retirement age.

If I stayed home, I wasn't necessarily giving up college. I could get an Associate's degree from Merlot Community College or maybe see if I could get into Sonoma State. Later, perhaps I could go to the Fashion Institute of Technology. My goal of being a fashion designer would just be a dream deferred.

My other choice was to follow my dreams to become a fashion designer, travel around the world, eat all the candy, and somehow have Tate in my life—this really special, wonderful guy. But freedom and fun would have major consequences. In that circumstance, I abandoned my parents, letting them fend for themselves, and cut off supporting them emotionally and physically.

So my choices? Be with my family. Or go to the college I wanted and have Tate.

I couldn't have both—not at once and not in the way I'd hoped for—because my parents needed me now and college could wait.

Problem was, I didn't know if my heart could wait. Or rather, if Tate would wait for me.

I *couldn't* be selfish and follow my dreams, and yet dammit, they were *my* dreams. There was a reason why I wanted to go to school to learn how to do the designs I loved, to travel and explore the world, and to be with the guy who I'd always ... *liked* a whole lot.

But leaving felt wrong. How could I choose anything other than what was right for my family—people who'd given me everything and who asked for me to do one simple thing in return?

Not liking the direction my thoughts had gone, after checking the mirror and making sure I was presentable, I entered the living room where my parents were watching TV. My mom held up the remote and fumbled to press the mute button so we could talk, since as usual they had the volume up to some huge decibel level.

"Let me do that, Mom," I said. I took the remote from her,

muted the television, and sat down beside her on the couch. I took her hand in mine and stroked it.

"How are you?" I asked.

"The usual." She sighed, giving me a wan smile. "I'm tired and frustrated. I want to have more energy, and I don't. And I don't want to be complaining about my ailments to my daughter. It's much more interesting to find out how you're doing."

I looked her over. She seemed normal, other than the visible fatigue that had seemed to plague her for months—tired eyes and graying hair. She certainly didn't seem any worse. "I'm excited to graduate," I said, which was true. "I've decided I'm going to apply to work on the wine train for the summer."

"That's a good idea, kiddo," Dad said approvingly. "Save up some money."

"That's my plan. Wren says they're hiring."

"How was it this afternoon with Tate?" she asked.

"Fun. We went to Black Bishop." I told her about the art, but I didn't mention the kissing. Or the fact that we were now boyfriend and girlfriend. I didn't want Dad to hang around in the hallway any more than he already did, since he was practically on patrol the last time.

My mom got a wistful look in her eye. "I'd like to go there."

"Dad and I should take you! It's really bright and fun. You should go."

Dad gave me a look. "I have to work the next few weekends."

"Well, we could go during the week—"

"Not if you're working on the wine train."

"I don't have that job yet. And I'm sure we'll find a good time to go."

But I couldn't argue them into having more fun, and the pressure of having to stay and justify to my parents why the things I did were good things for them to do too felt too much for me right now. Needing a breather already, I got up and went to the kitchen.

How was I ever going to make it through next year when everyone went off to college without me?

I closed my eyes and opened them again, gathering my wits. "Want me to make you popcorn, Dad? Get you guys something to drink?"

"Sure," he called. I felt relieved for something to do away from them, then guilty for that relief. If this was how it was going to be like after the summer, I didn't know if I'd survive.

I took the air popper out of the dishwasher.

Yes, the dishwasher.

Tim Staunton had his quirks, and he took a desire to not waste—money, water, time, or space—to maniacal levels.

He stored appliances in the dishwasher because he decided we never had enough dishes to run it and it was just basically a cabinet, so why not? We probably used enough dishes to fill it up daily but questioning Dad logic never went far.

Dad didn't only save weird things in the kitchen. He referred to his collection of plastic containers in the shower as the "bucket brigade." He hated wasting the cold water that came out of the shower before it heated up, so he used it on the begonias.

He removed the light from the vacuum cleaner to reduce energy usage. I tried to get him to explain to me exactly how much energy he'd save removing that bulb, but he wouldn't. Or couldn't.

I was pretty sure he still had the first dollar he ever earned locked away somewhere.

Is there any wonder his hobby was calculating what he needed to do to maximize his retirement?

I couldn't take away all his careful planning. Not with

someone who scrimped and saved as much as he did, in all the strange places.

He strolled into the kitchen just as the popcorn was finishing, whistling some song from the seventies while I poured juice.

"Dad," I said in a low voice. "I have to ask. About mom's care. Are there any alternatives? Or are the only choices either I have to stay and help you or you have nothing?"

He paused. "Those aren't the only choices. We could hire an aid or a home health nurse once she gets that far—bathing, eating, moving. Honestly, I think she's frightened about what's going to come, and she'll be more comfortable with family helping her. Not some stranger."

I nodded. "And how far out are you from retirement?"

He sighed. "To get the full amount, eighteen months."

I nodded again, calculating in my head. Summer, plus school year plus another summer. "Okay. So you really just need this year."

"Yeah, kiddo." He gave me a pained look. "I'm sorry to ask you to stay when we had it all planned for you to go to school. This isn't easy."

I needed to talk to Tate.

But discussing it with him would just make a hard decision even harder. And I couldn't let my dad or mom down.

I just couldn't.

Did that mean I'd made my decision?

Sometimes decisions were made without conscious thought. Because there was no other real choice.

We went back into the living room.

I handed my mom her drink and steeled myself to say the next part, because once I said it, I wasn't going back. "If you need me, I'll do it. I'll help out Dad and you. If I get a job on the wine train, I'll take classes here locally until Dad retires and I can transfer."

Relief washed over both of my parents' faces. And I knew I'd said the right thing. Made the only choice. I'd always pick my mom and dad.

Even if it broke my heart.

I bit my lip to stop it from trembling and wrapped my arms around myself to hold in the ache in my chest.

Tate and I could have this summer. After that?

Things weren't looking very good.

EIGHT

BOOK LEARNIN'

Still glowing after my date with Audrey, I walked into the kitchen, holding a plastic bag dangling from my fingers. I didn't know if it was better to hide my purchases behind my back or act like they were nothing. Though I wasn't that great of an actor, I decided to behave like they were no big deal. Maybe my family wouldn't ask. And if they did, I *had* purchased camouflage after all, so hopefully they wouldn't examine anything too closely.

Perry glanced up from by the sink, where he was shucking corn for Mom. Apparently we were having lobster boil for dinner, judging by the newspapers, spices, potatoes, and shellfish spread all over the counters. Lobsters listlessly waved their rubber banded claws from a container filled with water. Poor buggers.

"Hey," I called, as I walked in.

"Did you ace your oral?" Perry asked with a leer and a salacious wink.

"What?" I shook my head, not understanding. Then I set the bag down on the floor, walked over to where he was, and shoved him hard into the counter. Corn silk and husks flew everywhere. "Shut up, asshole."

"Oww. *Bastard*," he hissed, not unkindly, because he knew he deserved it. "Guess that means no." He bent down to pick up the corn husks, and I helped him. That shit went everywhere, and I hadn't meant to sully Mom's kitchen.

"Do I even want to know what you're talking about?" Mom asked as she cut and prepared potatoes.

"No," I said, at the same time Perry said, "Yes." Mom looked between us, confused.

I glared at my brother and then sighed in defeat. "I asked Audrey Staunton to go out with me. Officially."

The delight in my mom's eyes overtook her face, and she beamed. "That's wonderful news! I mean, I assume she said yes."

"Yes," I said. "She did." My skin tingled with happiness. Audrey was finally mine.

"'Bout time," Perry muttered. "I was about to ask her out myself."

A squawk escaped me. "Quit saying shit like that."

"Stop teasing the baby," Mom said.

I glared at her. "Jesus Christ, Mom. I'm eighteen. That's an adult. Not a baby."

She nudged my shoulder with hers, her hands occupied. "You'll always be my baby boy."

"Hey, what about this baby boy?" Perry asked, gesturing at his chest, back to shucking corn.

"Oh, you too, Perry," she said, to placate him. "You're my widdle baby, too."

He nodded, mollified.

I shook my head. "Need help?" I asked them, as usual.

"Nope," they both said, as usual.

Mom said, "Dinner in maybe an hour and a half," and I left

them, snagging my bag and heading to my room. They hadn't noticed my purchases.

After I dropped Audrey off at her house, where I gave her a quick peck and let her slide out the passenger side door—because otherwise I wouldn't ever leave—I drove to Barnes and Noble and hung out in the psychology section.

Which was located conveniently next to the sexuality section.

Which I knew beforehand, since I'd investigated a map of the store online.

Despite the talk with my brothers and a few online articles, I still needed specific information. Perry and Bert hadn't helped me plan my approach, and I was by nature a planner. I figured I'd buy *The Joy of Sex* or something similar to fill in the blanks. But as I stood in the aisles, my body placed closer to the psychology section than the sexuality section, I scanned the lurid pink, purple, and all-black covered books, getting increasingly discouraged by the titles.

I did not need a book on sex games. Nor on sexual dysfunction or how to connect with my lover after we'd been apart. Nor on premature ejaculation—at least I hoped I didn't need that—or *Viagra for the Soul*.

Where was *First Sex for Dumbasses*? Although truth be told, if that book existed, I wasn't buying it. Too embarrassing, and I wasn't a dumbass. Or rather, I hoped I wasn't.

I wanted something explaining what the hell to do with a willing woman in my bed and how to make being with me the best thing she'd ever experienced. Actually, I didn't want to know what to do with some generic woman. I needed to know how to make *Audrey* come. One specific, magnificent woman.

Could a book really be a substitute for experience? No, of course not.

But maybe I could get some practical tips—as much knowledge as possible—to make our first time amazing.

The worst thing that could happen would be I messed it up so much she'd leave me and never want to come back.

So, no pressure.

Once I'd inspected the meager sexuality selection multiple times, which was hard when you were pretending to be browsing in the neighboring section, my eyes latched onto a book called *She Comes First*. The title reminded me of Bert's advice, and it was the closest thing I'd seen on the shelf to what I wanted. Without wanting to linger anymore in the *SEX!* section of the bookstore, I snatched the slim paperback from the shelf, then picked up a bargain paleo cookbook from an end table as camouflage.

Carrying the sex book under the book on meat and veg, I walked through the huge store to the cash register, getting in line behind an old woman buying a pile of romance books and a kid with a stack of colorful children's books.

I did my best not to appear guilty. *Nothing to see here.*

A horribly familiar voice behind me said, "Hey! Tate! How are you?"

I slid the books to my hip and turned to Jade Lopez. I gave her a half smile. Then I grabbed a copy of Sports Illustrated to block the other side of the book.

"Never better," I said.

"Good, good. After graduation, I'm going to miss you. My mom's planning her birthday party this summer. It'll be in a few weeks. Do you think your mom would cater it?"

I wasn't listening. "Sure."

"Do you ever come to the tastings?"

Blinking, I fully faced her. "What tastings?"

"For catering."

"We don't normally do that. My mom develops a menu for each person, but she usually doesn't have samples."

"Oh." Jade's face fell. "I just thought I'd see you. Although you can come visit me at Penn."

Would she ever leave me alone? "Um," I said. "Maybe. Actually, I'm not sure—"

"Say, how come you never answer my texts?"

I wanted to tell her I blocked her number because I was dating Audrey, but then I heard, "Next!"

"See you around," I said, and hotfooted it to the register.

Face burning, I paid with cash, turning down the perky male cashier's kind offers to apply for a credit card and save ten percent because *Christ*, couldn't he shut up and let me out of this hellhole? I was pretty sure the cashier was onto me because he winked at me as I left. But whatever. I finished before Jade and speed walked to the MLR trying to make it look like I wasn't speed walking.

Now home, having survived the gauntlet of shoppers, Jade, cashier, and my mom and brother, I pulled the books out of the bag. I set the paleo one under my laptop to use as a stand, opened the magazine, and hid the sex book inside. Then I leaned back on my bed, my back against the headboard, and started reading.

Oh, *damn*. I picked the right one.

I read a chapter, then set down the book, the motion picture of the day running through my mind—Audrey sitting across from me at Craft, laughing with me at the winery, kissing me at the vineyard.

And I remembered how right she felt under me when we fooled around in the MLR.

Making out with her in the front seat of my truck was hot, but I needed to up my game. Maybe I'd rent a hotel, because we needed time and privacy. Although that wouldn't be for a while, because we weren't ready for going all the way yet. Just reading this book made me feel out of my league.

I read through the next chapter, and the next. I needed to quit before dinner because damn, this book turned me on, thinking of all the ways I could turn *her* on, which of course made my dick remember its earlier enthusiasm. It was definitely not happy with me for getting it all riled up again and not doing anything about it. But now was not the time. I couldn't very well walk into family dinner after just having jerked off. Though dinner with a hard-on wasn't much better.

How much time did I have?

I stuck my head out my door and yelled down to the kitchen. "Do I have time for a shower?"

"No," my mom called back. "Dinner in five."

Perry chuckled like he guessed what I wanted to do. Fuck him. Forget it. I put the book down and thought of everything disgusting thing I could think of to make the boner deflate. A few choice memories from Mrs. Sanchez's health class killed it for me. *Thank you, Mrs. Sanchez.*

I made it through the meal, helped with the dishes, excused myself from whatever my brothers were watching on TV, and returned to my room for the novel experience of being excited to study a new subject. Taking a deep breath, I opened the book again, finally getting past the introductory stuff and into the nuts and bolts part—so to speak.

Several hours later, in the middle of the night, I'd read the book the whole way through. And I was horny as all hell and had a *very* clear idea of how I could practice if I couldn't practice on Audrey.

The photo on the cover of the book had a papaya in the foreground, with a lonely little banana faded into the background. Cheeky, yes. But it gave me an idea.

Shirtless, with a boner raging in my gray sweatpants, I

snuck into the kitchen, hoping no one would see me and that my mom had some kind of melon she wouldn't miss. Or, hell, a papaya, not that I liked papaya. Fruit. I needed fruit. Because she was a caterer, we often had all sorts of random food around.

No one caught me headed into the kitchen, and *praise my mother*—although she could never, *ever* know what I intended on doing—I found a flat of ripe peaches on the counter.

No, I was not going to reenact *Call Me by Your Name* and beat off with the peach. Although now my brain was in the mode, it didn't sound as weird of an activity as when I first heard about it. It almost sounded sexy and fun. *Almost.*

But this peach had a different purpose, that of teaching dummy. I could learn to lick it.

Yes, I felt really fucking pervy.

I found three peaches, sliced them in half, threw away the pits, and set the fruit on a plate. I also grabbed a bunch of paper towels.

Then I slunk back to my bedroom and closed and locked my door. Feeling like a total dumbass from *First Sex for Dumbasses*, I put a peach on a paper towel on my bed. Then I lay on my belly, my hard cock grinding against the mattress, and positioned the fruit as if it were the area between her legs. I tested my tongue on it, giving it a careful lick.

Okay, it just tasted like a peach.

But I could do this.

Following the diagrams in the book, I practiced slow licks around the edges and long, rhythmic caresses with my fingers and my tongue.

This could be fun.

Problem was, instead of a peach, I was imagining my face between Audrey's legs. This book told me not to spread her legs far like in a porno, but instead to keep them close together, and I pretended her knees were over my shoulders. I kind of got into it, to tell the truth.

A knock sounded on my door, and I fucking freaked.

"What?" I said in an irritated and likely guilty voice, shoving a pillow over the peaches and closing the magazine over the book.

"What'cha doing in there?" called Perry, jiggling the door handle. I could hear the grin on the jerk's face.

"None of your fucking business," I growled, scrambling around for my T-shirt.

He rattled the doorknob again and thank god I'd locked it. "Which porn star are you watching, little bro?"

"Fuck off. None of them."

"So, can I come in?"

"No."

He laughed harder. "You sound kinda guilty, dude. You still a virgin after today?"

I'd had enough. "Leave me alone," I growled. "Unless you wanna join me."

That got him to leave. "Enough said." And I heard his footsteps pad down the hall as he chuckled the whole way back to his room.

Bastard.

With a hard dick and peach juice all over my face, I needed to shower, pronto. I'd had enough practice for the day. When the time came, I could do this.

I hoped.

Stripping off my clothes, I went into my bathroom, turned on the shower, and stepped into the warm water, prepared for a very fast beat-off session. Frankly, I'd had enough teasing today, from touching the curves of Audrey's body and getting a glimpse of her nipples, to knowing the way she tasted and getting to put my arms around her hot body. And now spending all this time with my dirty fantasies of her, I needed that release I earlier told her I could do without.

Water sluicing down my body, I gripped my cock and stroked hard, then came fast, gasping, wishing I could have the real thing.

Forever.

NINE

FINALS
AUDREY

I nestled in the dark blue pleather booth across from Wren at her mom's diner and put my knee up on the bench next to me. Because of finals, we'd gotten out of class early, and I'd joined her for lunch after school. Since we'd been busy studying all week, I hadn't really caught up with her, but some things I didn't want to put in a text.

Tate had some pre-graduation family thing to go to today. In a few hours I'd have to take my mom to the doctor's office because Dad was on shift. But for now I was enjoying the few moments I had with my best friend before I had to leave to pick Mom up.

Wren organized the sugar packets so they all faced the same way while I sipped on a root beer and doodled an outfit on a paper placemat. "I can't believe we're almost done with school. It's just ... over," she said.

"Almost. After tomorrow night." Our graduation would be Friday evening, and I both looked forward to it and dreaded it.

"Isn't it weird, though?"

"It feels anticlimactic. I hope I don't cry, though. That would be awful."

Mrs. Namuang stopped by our booth and set down our food. Wren had a bowl of soup while I had pad Thai and fries.

"Thanks," I said. "This looks tasty."

"Are you girls doing okay? I mean with life, not just with lunch?"

"Yes, Mom," Wren said. "We're just commiserating about graduation."

"Oh, it's a very important time," she said, a faraway look in her eyes. "Getting a diploma is a rite of passage. I am very proud of my daughter and you. It's an accomplishment."

"I suppose that's true," I said, doing my best to be polite, but wanting to dig into my lunch. "I think we're going to miss people from school though. For years we've been with them, and now it will be just ... nothing."

"You're going to see everyone anyway," she said. "Nobody really leaves Merlot. Not really."

"That's depressing," Wren said.

"It's a place to come back to after you go away," Mrs. Namuang said. "You need a home just as much as you need to know more about the world. You will see." She nodded gravely and walked off.

I turned to Wren. "That's the problem, though." I sighed. "I'm not gonna get to see more about the world for a long time. No Eurorail for me."

She gave me a sympathetic smile. "But you could be riding a train, right? Did you get the job on the wine train?"

I nodded. "They hired me almost immediately. I guess they're short-staffed and are going to be busy this summer. Plus my references were a caterer, a teacher, and a firefighter, so that looked decent." Sandra Lemieux, my English teacher, and my dad's coworker were the first people I could think of as references. "I have training starting late next week."

"Cool! I'm glad. Let me know how it goes. I hope you like it.

Allen Chen works there. Remember him? He was a senior when we were freshmen."

"Oh, yeah. He's a sweetie. I would've thought he'd go away for college."

"Nope. Or maybe he just works here in summers? I'm not sure."

"Ugh!" I whined. "People come here and never get out."

"You will," she assured me. "Eventually." Then a wicked gleam came over her face. "Soooo. We haven't talked. How's it going with Tate?"

"Fine."

She wouldn't let me get away with that answer. "Have you kissed him properly?"

I grinned and took a bite of noodles.

"Excellent," she said, clapping her hands. "Have you decided to let him deflower you?"

My hands flew up toward her face to shut her mouth, and she giggled. "Oh my god, keep your voice down. But yes."

"Well, well. That's exciting." She sipped a spoonful of broth. "Does Tate know this?"

I flushed. "We haven't exactly talked about it. I told him we could do whatever, though, so I think he gets the picture."

"Just make sure you talk to him, okay?" The concern in her face was unmistakable. "I mean, I want you to own your sexuality, but I also don't want you to get hurt."

"With Tate? Never. He's such a perfect gentleman."

"Really? I'd have thought he'd be sexy."

"He is," I said wistfully. I lowered my voice. "We finally made out for the first time, and it was *awesome*."

"I'm not gonna ask you for the highlight reel. But did you like it?"

I nodded.

"You do you, boo boo. But if you don't want to do him, you know you don't have to."

"I know," I said. "But I really, really want to."

"Don't get, like, obsessed with it, okay?"

"Don't worry," I assured her. "I won't." I raised an eyebrow. "I'm just hoping to get some experience in before he leaves for college. I told my mom I'd stay home for a year."

The thought made my chest tight and a headache start to brew.

"Have you talked with him about that?"

I shook my head.

She glared at me. "Why not? He deserves to have some say in this."

"What can he say, though? He can't fix my mom."

"But maybe he could work something out with you where you go visit him. You don't have to dump him at the end of summer."

"Is it fair to him to ask him to be long-distance? What if he resents me?"

"What if he doesn't?"

I shrugged, helpless. "I'll ask him, okay?"

"Make it soon. Someone is going to get their heart broken. He will, or you will. Or maybe you both will. And I don't want that to happen."

"I don't have a choice, Wren. I really like him. I don't want to stay away from him. He says he likes me. But I can't leave my mom." I felt my eyes start to well up with tears. "Tate is selfless. I'm scared he'll choose me, and I'm scared he won't. Neither choice is acceptable."

She clucked at me. "I think there's a lot more to it than that."

And I feared she was right.

A few hours later, I wrestled the new wheelchair out of the back of Dad's truck and awkwardly helped Mom get in. We'd practiced at home, but it was still difficult. Her brand new wheelchair had come just yesterday—Dad said it was a saga with paperwork and insurance—and it had given her more mobility, but it was also a reminder that the disease was progressing rapidly. I hated watching her get more and more frail. Maybe it had been sneaking up on us for a while and I hadn't noticed. Maybe I'd intentionally ignored the signs because I didn't want to process the changes. All the quiet conversations between my parents. The increased doctor's appointments. The prescriptions. The activities my mom couldn't do as well as she could before.

I couldn't ignore them anymore.

The wheelchair also reminded me that this was serious. So did the new parking placard. Mom needed me.

When we approached the reception desk to check in, I faced a familiar and very unwelcome face.

"Jade," I said. "Hey." I faked nonchalance.

I'd forgotten that Jade Lopez's mom practiced in the same office as my mom's doctor. And apparently since the last time I'd been here, Jade had been hired as a receptionist. *Great.*

My phone buzzed in my pocket with a text. I didn't pull it out.

"Audrey," she said with what I took to be faux surprise. She shouldn't have been surprised, though, if she saw my mom's name on the appointment list. But maybe she didn't put the two together. Or maybe she was showing off for my mom. "Welcome, Mrs. Staunton."

Jade clicked a few keys on her computer and told us Mom's copay, which my mother handed over.

"So," Jade said cattily. "I guess Tate talks to you."

"Yeah. He's always been my friend." Or now something more.

"I think he's ignoring me."

I don't care, Jade. I don't.

But I didn't want to be mean to her.

"So, Audrey. What are you doing this summer?" She pretended she was interested in me.

I did *not* want to chitchat with Jade Lopez. "Working. Helping my mom." *Making plans to take off my clothes while Tate takes off his clothes and rub myself all over his body.*

"Audrey got a job on the wine train," my mom volunteered, and I almost groaned. I didn't want Jade knowing anything about me.

"Oh? For the summer?" Jade asked innocently.

"Yeah. At least."

"When are you leaving for school?"

Of course she knew I was supposed to go to New York. The school was small, and we all knew each other's plans.

I didn't want to admit anything to Jade, but my mom did it for me. "Audrey's going to stay in town for the next year and defer the Fashion Institute of Technology. Once her dad retires, she can go. For now she's going to help me, so I'm sure she'll see you a lot more often."

I bit my tongue.

All Jade said was, "Interesting."

The nurse opened the door and invited my mom back. I followed her.

I leaned into my mom's ear. "Mom, I haven't told Tate yet. Can you please not tell people my plans until I tell him?"

Her face dropped. "Oh, honey. I'm sorry. I wasn't thinking. Of course."

We got into the exam room, and I pulled up my texts.

Tate: I have family in town this weekend. My parents and brothers are going to take them into San Francisco to see Ghirardelli Square and other tourist stuff, but I begged off

Tate: Wanna come over?

Alone time with Tate with no one around. I didn't have to think twice.

Audrey: Yes

And then I spent the entire appointment wondering what exactly we'd get up to when alone.

TEN

DON'T YOU DARE STOP

TATE

Holy shit. I'd get Audrey all to myself this weekend with no one to interrupt us.

That almost got my dick hard just thinking about it.

Her text felt off, though. No smiley faces or emojis. No enthusiasm. Just, "Yes."

But I'd take it.

Somehow, even though the world had changed for me and I had a girlfriend for the first time in my life, time marched on. We made it through Friday, the last day of school.

Before the ceremony that evening, I took pictures with Audrey in our caps and gowns, and we all clapped hard for her when she walked across the stage. My grandma and the rest of my family watched me stand up in a thin black gown and a cheesy cardboard hat covered in fabric and receive a piece of paper with my name on it.

We all graduated.

I didn't see much of Audrey after the ceremony, since she was doing her own thing with her parents. My extended family had come to celebrate, and my mom catered the fuck out of it.

All I could think about, for the first time, was that I really *was* biding my time to get Audrey naked this weekend.

No, that sounded wrong. I wasn't biding my time. I'd never bide my time.

But I knew that she and I wanted to do more, and since Black Bishop, we'd only had a few stolen kisses and hasty make out sessions in my truck.

So on Saturday when my whole family was out, she drove her dad's old truck over and knocked on my door.

"Hey," I said.

We were all alone.

"Hey," she said, a timid look on her face.

We couldn't have that.

I pulled her into my house and kissed her thoroughly in the hallway.

Then we grinned at each other.

I picked her up, and she wrapped her legs around me as I kissed her all the way down the hall to my bedroom. All natural, like we'd done that before. When we got to my room, I closed the door, locked it, set her down, and gazed at her.

Summer sun didn't touch her fair skin. Even though it was the weekend, she wore houndstooth shorts and a button-down top as if we were still in school, because that was Audrey.

She sat on the edge of my bed, her hands gripping the dark gray comforter. The Black Keys played softly, and to be honest, the tunes were kinda sexy music.

But Audrey looked nervous, biting on her lip, her shoulders clenched up.

And that made my next move easy.

We weren't doing anything. Not until she was ready.

I knelt before her, my shoulders between her legs and my hands on her thighs. I gazed up at her, wanting to reassure her.

"Hey," I said softly.

"Hey." Her expression was hard to read. Confusion? Desire? Fear? Comfort and discomfort all at once?

"We don't have to do anything. I promise."

The condoms in my drawer were wishful thinking on my part, and she didn't need to be pressured into anything.

"I know," she said, and sighed.

That sigh meant no.

So I started crab-walking backwards on my knees to give her some space, figuring I'd put a movie on my laptop, but she grabbed me and tugged me up to her.

I stumbled and ended up hovering over her, my hips between her legs and my hands braced on the bed. She put her hands on my cheeks and brought me in for a kiss. I went gladly and kissed her softly as her legs wrapped around my ass.

"I take it you want me to—" I started, and she clutched me tighter, moaning into my kiss. The quiet moan wasn't fake.

I made her feel that way.

"Touch me," she whispered. "Please."

Feeling brave, I moved a hand up her front from her waist and cupped one breast over her shirt.

One perfect breast.

"This okay?" I asked.

She nodded.

Maybe we'd just go slow. I decided to follow her lead.

I adored her breasts, the softness so unlike my own body. Her whole body was unlike mine.

And—er—so unlike the fruit I'd practiced on.

Our tongues tangled, and I found myself grinding into her. She didn't seem to mind. Actually, she seemed to be into it.

"This okay?" I asked against her mouth.

"Stop asking me if it's okay. It is."

"I want to be sure—"

"Tate, I trust you. Know that. Who else would take years to

kiss me? Only you. But we don't have time anymore, and you don't have to hold back anymore. Not with me."

I pulled back and tilted my head. "What do you mean?"

"I mean we don't need to wait years anymore."

There was something she wasn't telling me. Something I was missing.

Her movements took on a desperate quality, like she was trying to urge me on before I could say no, and I warred with myself. All I'd ever wanted was to be with her. But I also wanted to do things right. With her under me like this, I didn't know if I'd be able to take my time because I wanted her so fucking badly.

But I'd wanted her forever. I could wait a little longer.

Apparently that wasn't her plan, however, given how she gripped my dick through my jeans and gave a long, decadent stroke.

"Fuck," I hissed.

I started kissing down her neck, inhaling the strawberry scent of her thick hair and the almond scent of her skin.

She leaned into the bed away from me, and I got confused. Then she unbuttoned her shirt and whipped it off, and I was in love and lust all over again.

Her lacy bra was the sexiest thing I'd ever seen, although she could've worn a dingy cotton bra, and I'd have loved it.

"You're gorgeous," I murmured against her collarbone, kissing it. I reached back to the collar of my T-shirt and tugged it over my head. She eyed my torso with appreciation.

I pressed my body to hers, and now we were warm skin on warm skin, and *oh god more please*.

I didn't know if I trusted myself to do more. Or if I *should* do anything more than kiss her and feel her up.

But she started fumbling with the button on my pants, and I looked at her in surprise. "We don't need to rush."

"I want you." Her simple words hit me somewhere deep. She bit her lip, and I couldn't hold back anymore.

I started tugging on her shorts, but she reached down, unzipped, and slid them off.

She lay on my bed in nothing but her bra and underwear, her long, wild hair spread out like she'd already been debauched. Just like in my fantasies.

"Please," she whispered and beckoned me to come on top of her.

I didn't know what to do first. I decided to admit this to her. Because I could tell her anything.

So I whispered in her ear, "I want to be a sex god, but I've got no idea what I'm doing."

She smiled, and for the first time, she seemed relaxed. She stroked the top of my head with care. "That very thing—the fact that you tell me you don't know what you're doing—is what makes you a sex god. Because all that matters is that you listen to me. Truly. Everything else, we'll figure out. I just want to figure it out with you."

"I did some homework," I admitted. And I reached off to the side and pulled out the book.

Her breath intake was sharp, her eyes shrewd and calculating with some mischief behind them. "I can't wait to see what you learned."

I slid the straps of her bra down her shoulders, and she reached behind her to unhook it in the back.

Then she was topless, and I almost fainted. Those red nipples needed to be sucked, so I did. I kissed each in turn, then headed to her navel, kissing a path downward.

She struggled to sit up and see me. "What are you doing?"

I looked up at her from where I lay between her legs, my nose just below her bellybutton. "Want me to stop?"

"No. Just. I've never done that before." She threw her arm over her eyes.

I smiled and kissed her skin. "Me neither, but I'm dying to try. You good?"

She nodded vigorously, and I scooted down and kissed her between her legs over her panties. I inhaled her scent and had never been this turned on before. You couldn't smell porn—probably a good thing—and she didn't smell like the peaches I'd practiced on. Obviously. But I liked it a hell of a lot.

I kissed her pelvic bones and pulled her underwear off, then stepped back, just looking at her. She tried to hide herself with her arms, but I stopped her.

"Don't," I whispered. "Please let me see you. Let me remember this for the rest of our lives."

Her smile fell, and I didn't know why. I decided she needed affection. I crawled up her body, kissed her one more time on the lips, and drew her into my arms for a hug.

She clung to me.

Then she whispered, "Thanks. I really do trust you. And I want this."

I bent down to rub my nose against hers, and then we started kissing ravenously, like we couldn't get enough.

When we broke apart, I watched her. She seemed more relaxed. I drew my nose down her body until I got to the place between her legs, and I nuzzled it. I held out my tongue and took a tentative lick, and oh, god, yes, we needed to do this now.

She arched off the bed so hard, I wondered if I did something wrong. I glanced up at her in confusion, but her look was pure heat and lust.

I kept going.

I followed the book's instructions as best as I could remember, taking my time and letting her arousal build. After a while, I got brave and stroked her with a finger, then I slid it in.

"What did you put inside me?" she murmured.

"Just my finger." I was tempted to ask if she was okay, but I could listen to her instructions and trust her back. She'd tell me if she wanted me to stop.

In fact, she said the opposite. "That feels incredible. Oh my god, I love that."

"*You* feel incredible," I said. Because I loved her. But instead of saying it, I went back to licking her.

I could feel her squirming, and I wasn't sure if it was because she liked it or not, so I looked up and checked.

"Don't you dare stop," she moaned.

Okay, back to work.

The most pleasurable type of work there was.

I could say two things.

First, the book was awesome. Between the clues I knew to look for and reading Audrey's body, I could tell when she was about to come.

Second, when she came, her body became transfixed by some light, something in the future she couldn't see, could only feel. And it was so heavenly, I knew I wanted to see it over and over again.

So I did. Until she pushed me away and told me to stop. Just like the book said.

After she caught her breath, she smiled. "Are you going to, uh, fuck me now?"

I stilled. "No, baby girl. Not today."

"Can I go down on you?"

"I don't think I'll last that long," I admitted. "Why don't we just do, uh, a little hand work. Okay?"

She nodded and bit her lip, and I guessed this was the first time she was seeing a hard dick.

Shimmying my shorts and boxer briefs off, I lay back on my bed, letting her look at me. She ran her hands all over my body as I lazily stroked myself.

"Can I try?" she asked.

I nodded. "Hold it here," I said, showing her where I liked it.

And her small hand holding my big dick would officially be material to beat off to for the rest of my life.

When I came a few minutes later, with the accompanying mess, she looked almost as satisfied as me. "That was so hot," she whispered.

After cleaning up, I came back and cuddled with her until it was about time for everyone to come back.

Then she went home.

Bert was right, not that I'd ever tell him. Going down on my girlfriend was definitely the best first sexual experience.

I couldn't wait to do it again.

ELEVEN

TRAIN GOING NOWHERE

AUDREY

"Can you recommend something from the wine list?"

While the Napa Valley Wine Train rattled down the rails at only a leisurely four miles per hour, I still lurched toward the table I was serving, but I kept the fake, bright smile on my face as if I were just fine.

I'd pulled my hair back into a tight ponytail and wore a uniform of a crisp white shirt and black pants. I liked feeling polished, so that was on the plus side. Another boon to the job was the table crumber—the bent metal tool I kept in my pocket to scoop breadcrumbs off the table. Maybe I was weird, but I'd always liked those things.

"Let me have the sommelier come and discuss our selections with you. Anything else right now?"

They shook their heads, and I left with my head held high, trying to maintain my balance.

Carly laughed as I scooted past her in the aisle and whispered in my ear. "This would be a lot easier for you if you liked wine, you know."

I rolled my eyes.

My lack of wine knowledge probably hurt my tips, but I had a captive audience so I didn't do too badly.

At least not during these first weeks on the job. Weeks of evenings I'd spent setting up for the dinner service, serving it on a moving set of vintage train cars, then returning home and passing out from being tired.

Also, it had been weeks of sneaking kisses with my boyfriend. Of touching his body as much as I could. Of whispered promises against each other's skin. Of pushing whatever contact I could, because he left for Columbia in just a few short weeks.

But we'd had to sneak around. Except for the one lucky time no one was at Tate's house, we'd spent most of our touching in the front seat of the Mobile Living Room. Otherwise, we'd kept our hands to ourselves, talking as we usually did. Only we had an undercurrent of sex that was now brought to the surface. Actually, upon reflection, I think it'd always been there.

Tate texted me earlier today that his family was going out tomorrow night to some event and did I want to come over?

Hell yes, I wanted to come over. I didn't have to work tomorrow night, and apparently neither did he.

I arrived at the sommelier's station where Allen Chen had his twinky ass to me, checking the bottle inventory. "Table six needs you."

He turned around and gave me a flirty wink that didn't mean anything. Allen was more likely to hit on Tate. "I got ya, honey. I'll go see what they'd like." He sashayed down the moving train to help the diners pick a wine.

Continuing to the kitchen train, I put in the orders for table four and returned to the water station to get the pitchers. As I juggled the full water containers against the sway of the train, I did my best to not spill. When Wren mentioned this job, I hadn't fully realized the implications of serving fancy food and drinks on a *moving* train. The only thing worse than this would be to serve milkshakes while on roller skates. But I did my best.

The Napa Valley Wine Train was world-renowned for its incredibly elegant dining. The silverware was real silver, polished and precise. The dinner screamed "chef-fy." And the view—

Well, it was home.

Here's a secret. Don't go on a scenic wine train excursion at night in winter. Because there's no view in the dark. You're welcome.

But on a lovely July evening like tonight, the late sun shone on the green rows of vines and bright mustard growing in between the rows. The vintage cars trundled down the tracks along the different viticulture districts. Rutherford. Yountville. And so on.

The beauty didn't change the fact that the only train I got to ride on went nowhere.

Carly sidled up to me once I returned the pitcher to its place and checked on the rolls. "Going out with Tate tonight?"

"No, he has to work. But we're getting together this weekend."

Tomorrow night, I told myself. Tomorrow night, Tate and I would finally do it.

I texted him.

Audrey: There's so much I want to do to you. You have no idea. I have a list

Tate: Is it an Anti-Bucket List?

Audrey: Even better. A secret list

And I hummed the rest of my shift.

When I saw him the following evening, I attacked. In so many words.

Once I confirmed we were alone, I shut the door behind us and fused my mouth to his.

Then I climbed him like a tree. Like he was the Empire State Building and I was King Kong.

At first, he gave back as good as I gave and more, but then I got frantic. Because if this was the only time I had with him, I was going to make the most of it. We had to move. We couldn't stay still.

He pulled back, giving me a blue-eyed smirk. "Whoa. Slow down. We have all the time in the world. I'm not going anywhere, baby. I just want to be with you."

But I wasn't listening. I was kissing. I slid down his body and started pulling his shirt up and then tugging at the fly of his pants as we shuffled to his bedroom. "I don't have all the time in the world. I don't want to wait."

"Patience."

"No," I said. "*Im*-patience."

"Audrey, I want you so much, but I want to know every inch of your body, and I don't want to skip any steps."

What I wanted to say was, "But I want you nowww."

Instead, I looked at the ground, keeping a sigh from escaping. I wasn't being very adult. And if I was having sex, I needed to be an adult.

His eyes sought out mine. "What's this about, Audrey? Because I'm as horny—or probably hornier—than you are, but I want this to be special." He smiled, a glorious full smile. "Because it's you. I want it to be special with you. I don't want to go fast and get it over with. And I'm not sure I'm ready."

He didn't say, "I'm not sure you're ready either," but I heard it in his tone.

I sighed for real. He was right.

Worse, my plan wasn't fair to him in the slightest.

I still hadn't told him I wasn't going to New York. Every time I wanted to bring it up, it didn't feel like the right moment. But the longer I waited, the more difficult it became to bring it up.

Because I was falling for him. Or in truth, I'd fallen a long time ago.

And the physical distance we'd have would be painful. I didn't know if it would be more painful to ask for long-distance or if it would be better to just break it off.

And I didn't want to ask.

For now, we ended up making out and feeling each other up. He kissed me, and it felt different than our last time in his bed. That time felt like we needed to break through some barrier just to say we passed it. Tonight, we didn't have that pressure. We spent our time together exploring new territory. Instead of zipping past on an airplane overhead to get to another city, we traversed the terrain of each other.

And it was ultra sexy.

I memorized his torso, finding a little freckle on his left side, and learning he wasn't as ticklish as I was. My lips traveled along the hollows of his neck and the sculpted parts of his collarbone.

In return, he put his mouth on every single part of me. Seriously. He kissed me behind my ear and along my neck down to my fingertips, then kissed my palm and all the way on up my inner arm. Then he repeated it on the other side, as if he too was mapping my body. Reverently.

"Yeah," I said on a happy sigh. "This is better."

"I have a present for you," he said. And he pulled out a small gift bag.

I had no idea if he was giving me lingerie or a sex toy or

something naughty, but it ended up being a couples' massage oil that smelled divine.

From our make out session, our shirts were off. But we took everything else off.

He got on his belly, and I rubbed the oil between my hands, then straddled his back and used it on his naked shoulders, all the way down to his perky ass. As I massaged every part of his back, he moaned in pleasure. And I kissed as much of him as I could reach.

He returned the favor. Low lights. Quiet music. And his broad hands all over my back. Seeing me, really seeing me.

We didn't have sex, at least not anything penetrative. But he brought me to an orgasm, his intense eyes watching me, and then I watched him do it to himself per my request.

I thought that it didn't matter if I landed in Merlot or New York or Stockholm or Kiev. If I had Tate in my life, it was enough.

TWELVE
BORING PARTY WITH DECENT CATERING
TATE

I hoisted the tray of goat cheese canapés and wended my way through the crowd. It was a pretty party—a fiftieth birthday celebration—but it didn't matter who attended this shindig because I was on the clock and not here to socialize. In the summer evening at the edge of a vineyard, a Beatles cover band played near a white tent. Strings of large white lights draped over the outdoor dance floor, and white roses sat on tables covered in white tablecloths.

I yawned.

At least they'd hired a decent caterer, but the decor was as blandly pretty as it could be.

Or maybe it just lacked the spark of a certain redhead.

I had a job to do. With a smile, I offered the hors d'oeuvres to guests in gauzy dresses and pastel polo shirts.

Until my smile fell when I ran into a familiar face. Jade Lopez stood before me, wearing a dark blue linen dress and high heels.

"Hey," I said, not wanting to be rude. I set down the tray of hors d'oeuvres on a nearby table and brushed off my hands. Somehow I'd ended up at the edge of the party. I glanced around for an exit, but to escape her, I'd have to push through the crowd and make a scene. I sighed, cornered. "What are you doing here?"

She took a step toward me. I had to keep myself from taking a matching step back. "It's my mom's birthday," she cooed. "I'm glad you could come."

"Ah. I'm, uh, just here to work for my mom. I'm not a guest."

"I know. We talked about it at Barnes and Noble."

"Ah, that's right." I'd totally forgotten.

"You'd know that if you answered my texts," she said.

"About that—"

"Still, you're here. And that's all that matters." She took another step toward me, and I wished I hadn't set down the tray. I needed a buffer.

"I need to—"

"Tate. Why don't you see if you can stay after the party. We have a guest house. It's very private. We can, you know. Hang out." And the way she said it left no doubt as to what she meant.

I stared at her. "No. After this I have to go—"

Before I could do anything, she wrapped her arms around my neck and kissed me.

It felt all wrong. Wrong girl, wrong lips, wrong place. Just no.

I stood there in shock before I recovered, unhooked her arms that encircled my neck, and stepped back. "Jade, look. You have to leave me alone. I'm not interested in dating you. Audrey and I are together."

A wicked look came over her face. "For now. When you go to Columbia, you won't be seeing her. I'll be close at Penn. I can come visit."

"No, she's coming with me to New York. I'll be spending most of my time with her."

She gave me the evilest grin I'd ever seen outside of a Disney villain. "Oh, Tate. Audrey isn't going to New York."

A sinking feeling in my gut outpaced the sudden headache I was getting. "What the hell are you talking about?"

"She's staying in Merlot to take care of her mom." Jade's face said innocent, but I knew she was anything but. And I was trying to figure out how I could wipe off her kiss discreetly.

I narrowed my eyes at her. "How do you know about that?"

"I see Audrey every week when she takes her mom for her appointments, and she told me all about her plans. I don't know why she didn't tell you." Again, the faux innocence. I just needed to throttle her.

But her words made me pause.

I knew Mrs. Staunton had been diagnosed with MS. Audrey had told me before, and she'd talked about going with her to doctor's appointments.

But Audrey staying in Merlot?

Jade was still talking. "I didn't know you had no idea. I thought she would have told you she wasn't going to New York with you."

Not going to New York? What the actual fuck?

God, Jade was such a conniving bitch.

But what if Jade was telling me the truth? Because if she'd seen Audrey's mom, maybe she did know what she was talking about.

If Audrey wasn't going to New York, I couldn't … breathe.

"I have to go," I blurted, not waiting to see Jade's reaction, and took off with my tray the long way to the prep area. Once there, I set down my tray and found my mom.

"Do you have enough coverage tonight? Something's up with Audrey and her mom. It's important. Can I go?"

She nodded, surely seeing my wild-eyed expression. "Tate? What's wrong?"

Why wouldn't Audrey tell me?

"I don't know, Mom. I need to find out if Audrey is alright."

Did she not trust me?

"Yes, of course you can go. Let me know. I hope she's okay." She paused and wiped what was assuredly lipstick off the side of my mouth. "What happened?"

"Long story."

"Then go."

And I ran to my truck and raced to her house.

Audrey opened the door with a surprised expression. "Tate? What are you doing here? I thought you were working."

"I left early," I said. "I wanted to talk with you."

She looked over her shoulder into the dining room where her parents were seated.

"We're just sitting down for dinner," Chief Staunton said. "Want to join us?"

I took a deep breath. "Yes."

THIRTEEN

GUESS WHO COMES TO DINNER

For the first time ever, Tate sat as the fourth person at our dining room table, helping himself to my dad's cooking. He was so big he dominated his side, balancing out my dad.

It actually felt comfortable having him here, although his worried expression bothered me.

Thankfully, my dad had made tacos and not pork chops. I couldn't survive Tate having to eat my dad's pork chops. Especially given his mom's profession.

"It's nice to have you here, Tate," my mom said.

"Thanks. I wasn't planning on crashing your dinner, but it's good timing. I've been working all evening and haven't stopped for a break."

I passed him the salsa. "How was the party?"

"It was fine." He sipped his water. "Actually, it was Dr. Lopez's birthday party."

My stomach sank. "Oh?"

"Yeah." His voice went husky, and he passed me the taco meat. "I talked with Jade."

"How did that go?" I asked, knowing I sounded anything but nonchalant.

"She said you weren't going to New York this fall."

I closed my eyes and opened them to see my mom and dad watching each other warily.

"Audrey," my dad said. "You haven't told him?"

"Are you not going to the Fashion Institute?" Tate's voice cracked.

"Tate," I said, doing my best to keep my voice calm and to not tear up. "I have to stay and take care of my mom."

All sorts of emotions flitted across Tate's face. Anger. Sadness. Regret. "So it's true." He turned to my mom. "Mrs. Staunton, are you doing okay?"

"Oh yes," she said. "It's new, but I'm managing. This disease is my new companion. I'll just have to learn to deal with it."

"It's not fatal," my dad said, and Tate let out a relieved sigh. But then he swiveled to me, his eyes hard.

"Why didn't you say anything before? We had all these plans—"

"Because I was scared of what you'd say."

My mom and dad watched us like a tennis match, and I couldn't handle the audience.

"Can you excuse us?" I asked.

I stood up, and Tate followed me to my room. I closed the door, trusting my dad wouldn't come knocking.

I took a deep breath and faced Tate. He held up a hand. "I have to tell you. Jade kissed me."

This stopped me from saying what I intended. "*What?*"

"I'm not keeping anything from you. At the party, she made a pass at me. I didn't kiss her back."

He told me what happened. That *bitch*. But Jade touching Tate was minor compared to what I'd done.

I took a deep breath. "I'm sorry Jade touched you. But I'm sorrier that I didn't come to you first. I've been trying to figure out a way to talk with you about this."

"Audrey," he said. "You can talk with me about anything."

"Not about this."

"Why not? It involves me. It involves *us*."

"Because you're not the only one who likes to figure out everything in advance. And this problem doesn't have a solution. If I can just hold out for the school year, Dad receives his full retirement. They asked me to help out." I dropped my eyes. "I couldn't say no."

"So, that's what you're doing? Delaying for a year."

I nodded, not trusting my voice. But I managed to say, "Because he can't take care of her by himself. I have to help my family."

"And you decided this without talking to me."

It wasn't a question. I sighed. "Tate. You can't solve this. You can't buy your way out of this. You can't change my dad's retirement age. You can't make her better. There's no solution."

Tate closed his eyes then opened them. Then he went to the door, his hand on the knob. "I'm sorry your mom is sick. Truly."

"Me too." I squeezed my eyes shut.

"But I don't understand why you didn't talk to me about this. You just assumed, what—that we'd have to break up? We could figure something out. I can stay home—"

I held up my hand. "No. See? That's what I didn't want. I knew you'd offer something like that. And I can't make you give up New York."

"Why didn't you *ask* me what I wanted?" The hurt in his tone chastened me. "Because all I want is you."

I'd fucked up.

And tears really began to stream down my face.

"All I want is you, too. And I can't have you."

"I'll stay," he said.

"No. I can't ask you to do that."

"I'd do it for someone I love."

His words made my insides seize up. Tate loved me.

"I love you, Audrey. But this is a two-way street. We have to be able to talk. If you don't feel like you can talk with me, then maybe our relationship isn't what I thought it was."

"It is," I said quickly. "I just couldn't figure out a good time to tell you."

"So you settled on not telling me?"

I didn't have an answer to that.

He faltered, his eyes imploring me. And then apparently resigned because he must not have seen what he wanted to see in my eyes. "You know what? I need to go home."

Giving me one last look, he opened the door and walked down the hallway. I heard him say thank you to my parents.

Then the front door closed and the MLR drove away.

When I stepped back in the dining room, red-faced and tearstained, my parents didn't say anything. I opened my mouth, but no words came out.

"Oh, honey," my mom said. "I'm sorry."

"It's not your fault you're sick."

But I couldn't eat anything.

Later that night, I texted Wren.

Audrey: Tate found out about me staying home this fall

Wren: What happened?

Audrey: He was upset

Wren: <Unhappy face emoji>

Audrey: You were right

Audrey: I should have talked with him

Audrey: It sucks

Audrey: I hurt him

Audrey: And I feel awful
Wren: I wish I could make it all better

I was headed for bed when there was a knock on my bedroom door. My mom wheeled in. "Can we talk?"

I nodded.

"I'm sorry."

"Mom. Don't be sorry. It's not your fault. It's just the way things are. You'd take care of me if I were sick, and I'll take care of you. Don't worry about it at all."

She gave me a watery smile and held out her shaking arms. I threw myself into them, holding her tight. Her feeble hug made up for its lack of vigor by letting me stay in her arms for a long time.

When she wheeled herself out of my room, she paused and gave me one last glance over her shoulder. "I love you, Audrey."

"Love you too, Mom."

On my desk was an official-looking envelope I'd received in the mail today. I opened it up and almost choked.

My passport. I'd forgotten that Tate had paid for it to be expedited. He wanted us to be able to go travel at any time.

My picture inside looked like I was having the time of my life, probably because I was. Because he'd given me the present of possibility.

The blue passport pages were shiny, with holograms on them. And so many blank pages. I didn't know if they still stamped passports or not but I wasn't finding out any time soon.

Tate was going to show me the world. But with how hurt he was when he left, now I didn't think that would ever happen.

FOURTEEN

FULL MR. PEANUT

Sitting in my bedroom, I pulled the folded piece of paper out of my wallet that had our Anti-Bucket List on it. Ever since we wrote it, I'd been carrying it around with me. Toy store in New York City and clothes shopping in London. Food and celebrations and trains.

But it didn't matter, because it wasn't going to happen.

What hurt more was that Audrey had been holding this inside, unable to tell me. I had to find it out from Jade fucking Lopez, someone who had no business telling me.

Holding the folded piece of paper in my fingers, I went to tear up the list, but paused. I couldn't bring myself to do it. My heart couldn't take it.

I was pissed, yeah. But I also was hurt she didn't think we could work this out together. Was something else going on? Had Audrey been using me? For what, I didn't know.

I thought back on all the smiles she'd given me and all the support in school and otherwise. How delighted she seemed just to be around me. How many hours we spent together doing nothing or anything in particular.

How good she felt with her body next to mine.

No, our relationship had to mean something to her. She'd admitted she liked me. And she was genuinely crushed.

Maybe I wasn't being fair.

I thought about what I'd do if my mom got sick, and I knew the answer. Like Audrey, I'd do anything for her. Even give up my dreams.

I felt bad now for being selfish and wanting Audrey all to myself. Because she'd never be just mine. She had family and friends and school and work and other people in her life. Our life couldn't consist of only the two of us on some train traveling somewhere. We needed to *live*, but it didn't really matter how we did that.

What I needed was another plan.

If I had to stay in Merlot to be with her, I would. If she had to defer, I would, too.

That's not what she wanted you to do, I reminded myself. *She knew you'd act that way, and she wanted you to not to.*

But I had to fix this.

When I walked in the den, my brothers sat watching another Giants game.

Despite my mood, I choked out a laugh. Perry wore the monocle in his eye and a pipe clamped in his mouth.

"So you're really going full Mr. Peanut?"

"You got it, little bro."

I shook my head. "You're such a weirdo."

"Better to be a weirdo than to be boring."

They took one look at my face, then at each other.

"You still a virgin?" Perry said.

Bert nodded. "He still has that glow. Like a unicorn. Innocent."

"Leave me alone," I said. And then, "She's going to break up with me. I know it."

My grouchy mood showed, and I slumped onto the couch. Bert passed me a soda.

And I told them everything.

When I finished, Bert asked, "How are you doing?"

"Okay," I said, but it felt like a lie.

"Bullshit," Perry said cheerfully. "You're in a funk."

I shrugged. "Maybe."

"Maybe? Let me gather this. Your girlfriend is staying here, and you're going away to college. She's maybe broken up with you because she didn't want to do long distance. Oh, and you're still a virgin."

I nodded.

"And you're in love." Bert added helpfully.

I nodded again.

"You know I was only ever kidding about dating her," Perry said. "I mean, she's hot, but she's clearly yours."

I looked up at him in surprise. "Thanks for saying that."

"I mean, if you dump her, give her my number."

As usual, I growled.

We watched the game. I went and got us snacks after a bit, and when I returned, Perry and Bert looked at each other and nodded.

"We have an idea," they said at the same time.

"You two are creeping me out."

"No, it's a great idea," Perry assured me.

And as I listened, I thought they were onto something.

Maybe this could work.

FIFTEEN
SACRIFICES
AUDREY

The next day, Tate texted me saying he was sorry he left in a hurry, and he wanted to figure out how to make this work.

I love you, my fingers typed. But I didn't hit send.

I tried to be optimistic, but I didn't see a solution.

Still, a gift bag was on our porch this morning with my mom's name on the tag. It had a soft blanket, a special cushion to sit on, comfortable slippers, and cashmere socks.

A lump formed in my throat.

Tate's language of love was gifts. And he was telling me he loved me and supported my decision to help my family by giving my mom presents.

That made me take to my room the entire morning.

At dinner, my parents studied each other. Then they both looked at me.

"Pork chops," I said, trying not to be sarcastic. "Yum."

Pretty sure I failed at keeping the sarcasm away. We were having an early dinner because I had to scoot to get to work.

"Audrey," my mom started. "Are you happy?"

I shook my head. "I'm sorry, but I'm not. I wish it didn't

matter. Going to college. Or ... anything else." I let out a breath. "I love you guys. I'll stay as long as you need me."

"And we love you," my mom said. "But there are other things to consider."

I shoved a bite of meat in my mouth and swallowed, trying not to choke down the dry texture. "Don't worry. I'm not complaining. I choose you, Mom."

She reached a trembling, slim hand over to me and touched my wrist. I stilled. Her eyes caught mine. "I know, honey. But your dad and I were wrong."

I wasn't having any of this. "No, you weren't. Family matters. You can't talk me out of it."

"Tate matters, too."

I gulped.

"Do you love that boy?"

I nodded. Because it was true. "Always. He's the best person I've ever met."

"Then you should go to school with him."

"No—"

"Audrey, that boy loves you. We should never have asked you to stay home."

"Mom, I'm not leaving you. I made my decision. It's acceptable."

She stared at me. "But is that true?"

I stared back. And her eyes broke me. "No, it's not. He's the love of my life. I want to be with him for the rest of my life. I know I'm young, but we've been taking this so slowly, we've built our relationship on a solid foundation. But Mom, I don't want to lose you."

"You will. It's a fact of life. And I'm not going to chain you to this house when you're in the prime of your life. You should be out there learning what it is you like."

"And I told you, I'm willing to give that up to help out."

"It is for the parent to sacrifice for the child. Not the child to sacrifice for the parent."

"Um, Mom. Not true. Children sacrifice for their parents all the time. I'm willing to do whatever you need."

"But I'm not willing to accept it anymore."

I gaped at her. "I'm not going to make Dad figure out how to do all of this with working at the station too."

"Actually, kiddo," he chimed in, "your mom and I had a long talk last night. I'm going to retire."

"But you can't—"

"If I wanted to take the full amount of my pension, yes, I need to stay in longer. But I did the math. And no math on the planet is enough for me to miss the time with my wife or hinder my daughter's education or love. We're applying for disability, too. Your mom should qualify. So I'm retiring."

I burst into tears, wiping my eyes with the back of my hands.

"And besides, I'm a frugal kind of guy. You know we'll be fine."

"Your dad and I are telling you that we think you should go live your life the way you want to. Not the way we asked you to." Mom's eyes shone with love.

"I'm willing to do anything for you," I said helplessly.

"Then live a full and complete life."

"I've deferred FIT already."

"Well, maybe you can ask them to take it back. Work with them. Or maybe you spend the year doing things you want to do."

I nodded, needing to get up. To move. To do something. "Would you excuse me?"

She smiled. "Do you have a boy to call?"

"I think I need to go over there. I might be able to find him before work. I need to talk to him."

"Go get him," said Dad.

I nodded, grabbed the keys to Dad's old truck, and headed up to the highlands of Merlot.

When I got to Tate's house, Perry answered the door wearing a silk vest, houndstooth trousers, and a newsboy cap.

"Is Tate here?" I said breathlessly. "Also, can I take a picture of you? I might need to use you as design inspiration."

He grinned. "Yes, to both." Then he stood back, let me snap a pic, and called over his shoulder, "Tate, your booty call is here!"

"Oh my god!" I yelped and shoved his shoulder. "Don't say that!"

But he stepped aside and let me pass. I trotted down the corridor to Tate's room, where I hoped I could find him, Perry right behind me.

His room was empty.

"Well, I thought he was here."

"I only have a few minutes before work." I whipped my head around wildly. "Do you know where he went?"

"No," Perry said. "Sorry, I don't know where he is."

"Well, if you see him, can you tell him to call me? It's really important."

He nodded. "Sure thing, girlie."

I turned on my heel and ran back to the truck. I had to make a decision—change in the car or change somewhere at work—so I stripped quickly in Tate's driveway, hoping no one watched, but not having enough time to care.

The white shirt slammed over my head, and I got caught in the sleeve.

"Gah!" I yelped. I shoved down my shorts and threw a leg

into the black pants. Yanking them up over my ass, I got them on. I fired up the old truck and put it in reverse, driving too fast across the windy road from Sonoma over the hill to Napa. I made it just in time. I slid into a parking spot and ran up to the train, getting ready to start my shift.

"Hey!" Carly said. "Where's the fire?"

"It's been a crazy day," I said. I ran to the cars, to get the tables set for the dinner service.

God. All I wanted to do was talk to Tate. I should text him, but I wasn't allowed to use my phone while working. I needed to be responsible. I'd do my job, then find him the moment I got off work. Hopefully the wait wouldn't kill me.

An hour and a half later, the train started to load passengers, and I waited at the sommelier's station with Allen talking about the differences between syrah and merlot wines.

"Grapes," I said. "They're different grapes."

He gave me a grin. "Good. Now go take care of our diners."

The train started, and I headed to my car. I greeted the first table of diners, but then out of the corner of my eye, I saw a table at the end of the car with only one diner.

A familiar diner.

A diner with cornflower blue eyes and sandy blond hair.

A boy on the train. Waiting for me.

SIXTEEN

BOY ON A TRAIN

AUDREY

I finished with the table, asking them to tell me their choices three times because I couldn't concentrate, then skipped the next table to talk to Tate.

When I stood in front of him, I choked out a sob. "You're here." All I wanted to do was fall into him and let him catch me. I wanted to talk to him and tell him what my parents had said, but I had a job to do.

He smiled at me with his perfect pouty lips and kind eyes. Those eyes so full of love and compassion.

"Tate. I'm sorry—"

"Shh, no," he said, patting my hip comfortingly. "Go do your job. We have plenty of time to talk when you're done."

I wiped my face and gathered myself, nodding repeatedly. "Okay. I can do that."

Carly sidled past me and did a double take. "Wait, is this Tate?"

"Yes."

She looked between us. "Go to the staff car. No one's in there right now. I'll cover for you."

I gave her a grateful smile. "Thank you." Turning to Tate, I said, "Let's go."

He stood and followed me. We made our way through one car to the next, going through the space between cars and opening the vintage doors. When we finally got to the staff car, I turned to him and looked up. "I'm so sorry—"

He grabbed me and hugged me, and I'd never felt anything better than his arms. "Shh, babe. No. Don't be sorry. Next time be up front with me. I can handle your truths. And you wanted to take care of your mom. That's *good*. It's noble and selfless."

"But I didn't want to give you up," I said. "I wanted to be with you, and I couldn't, so I panicked. Because I couldn't hurt you. I wanted you to have the full life you deserved and not to be stuck with someone from this dinky little town."

"We can have a full life together," he said, and tucked my hair over my shoulder.

"My parents said I can go to school."

"Really?" His face shone with happiness.

I nodded and explained what my parents had said. "I have to see if I can rescind my deferment."

"If that doesn't work, I might have something better. Bert and Perry came up with an idea. And I ran it by my parents."

"What's your idea?" I asked, my heart racing.

"A gap year."

"What?"

"In Europe, lots of people take a year after they graduate from high school to travel and figure out what they want to do before they go to college. I'll defer Columbia, and you and I can travel the world."

My heart soared and took a nosedive. "I don't have the money for that."

"Don't say no, Audrey. Figuring out how to do this is half

the fun. I'll sell my truck, and we're both working. You've saved your money, right?"

I nodded.

"I think we can do this."

Hope began to blossom in my chest. "Are you serious? You'd do that for me? Hold off on school?"

"I'd do that for *us*, yeah. And we can stay in town and help your mom as much as you want, then go travel and return as she needs. We can schedule around your dad. Although if he's retiring—"

"Then we can do our list."

And with that, he bent down and kissed me. And even though there was no view, no sunset, no setting. It was wonderful. Game changing, again.

"I have to tell you something," I said, once we broke apart, breathless. "I'm completely and totally in love with you. I don't know when it started, but it's been a very long time. I was just too scared to act on it or to say anything. I was stupid."

"Don't you dare call yourself stupid," he said. "We just took our own time. We were on our own schedule."

"Yeah," I said. "Maybe we were. Maybe we have been."

"Maybe we'll continue to do that." He grinned. "And I love you, too."

I grinned at him. "Hungry for some dinner?"

"I thought you'd never ask."

SEVENTEEN

FINALLY

I leaned in to kiss Audrey.

I had to. I had to touch those strawberry lips with mine. To feel their softness and to taste her sweetness.

It'd been weeks since I met her on the train. I knew she'd never been to Disneyland. Well, we couldn't have that. So after a full day of rides and a lovely dinner, we entered our suite at the Grand Californian Hotel.

Her lips parted, and she inhaled sharply. "I want you."

Hell.

I trembled.

Our lips crashed together like it was inevitable.

Because it was. We belonged together.

Tate Lemieux and Audrey Staunton were supposed to be together. It had been written in the stars. No, more like we wrote it in our high school yearbooks, in all those photos of us with each other, smiling. Even when we were just friends.

Although I don't think we were "just" friends. Too small a term for how big I felt about her.

We'd spent weeks exploring that big feeling. Instead of

rushing into sex, we'd held back. Learning each other's bodies as well as we knew our own.

But now it was time. We were both ready.

My tongue touched hers, and we got tangled together. Her breasts smashed against my chest, and she grabbed my ass, squeezing it with some serious fondling, and it made me hard.

Harder.

God, I wanted this girl.

"Please," she whispered against my lips. "Please make love to me."

I nodded into her neck. "My pleasure." My heart beat a fast tattoo.

Slowly, I reached down to the hem of her shirt and tugged it up over her body.

She stood before me in a lavender lace bra, not hiding from me anymore.

"Match me," she said.

I did. I shucked off my T-shirt, pulling it from the back of my neck over my head, and stood before her barefoot in my jeans. I slid my belt out, and my jeans dropped low on my waist so you could see the tendons wrapping around my hips.

"Ungh," she said, sliding her hands up my torso. "I like this. So, so much."

I pulled my phone from my back pocket and scrolled for a David Bowie song. When I pressed play on "Lazarus," I put it back and gestured toward her. "C'mere."

Gathering her in my arms, I began to dance with her, kissing her deeply while our bodies moved.

And as we danced, I slid my hand down the back of her ass, feeling the roundness of her ass. Feeling how small and curvy she was. How lovely and sleek and *mine*.

Then she reached in front and unbuttoned her tweed pants. She unzipped them and danced them off.

She wore matching lavender lace cheeky panties that framed her pale hips, and I murmured my appreciation when my hands gripped her velvet skin.

I unzipped, shoving my jeans down, and we were dancing in our underwear—her in lace, me in new Tom Ford boxer briefs.

My hard dick pressed against her smooth belly, and I hoisted her up. She wrapped her legs around me, and I continued to move. I walked over to the bed, laying her down. Wiggling and giggling and singing along, she clung to me while I danced in a horizontal position, which incidentally made my dick dig into her.

She gasped, and I loved it.

She loved it, too.

The song stopped, and a new one started—"Heart of a Dog" by the Kills—and she sighed into my neck. "I love this song."

We rolled over and she straddled me. "I love this view."

I reached up and moved her panties to the side. I could rip them off, but I thought it was sexy to keep them on.

My fingers found her center, and she was aroused and wet. I dove in, keeping up the rhythm. She ground on my fingers, losing herself.

Exactly what I wanted her to do.

Then she moved to my cock, rubbing against it.

God, yes.

She tugged my hair and pulled me up to kiss her, which I did very deeply. Then I flipped her to her back.

Her bra unhooked in the front—*love this kind*—and I flicked it open. I let her boobs loose, and I was mesmerized.

"Oh, god," I groaned as I kissed her bare skin. "You're so sexy."

She grinned. I hung my thumbs on the panties, and she let

me slide them off. Then she was bare. Naked. On the bed. Waiting for me.

I wanted to keep my underwear on, because I'd be tempted to just shove inside her if I didn't have anything on. But I wanted to make sure she came before I made love to her.

And it would be making love, because I was so in love with her I couldn't bear it.

With my fingers between her legs, I kissed her neck, then looked up and watched her eyes flutter shut and her body sink into the sensation.

I massaged her with more intent, kissing her collarbone, sucking on her tits. Wanting to make sure she came.

My movements weren't necessarily what the books and articles said to do.

They were what I'd learned drove my Audrey wild.

I could feel how her clit changed. How she was soaked with arousal.

And I kept it up. I could tell she was getting close. If I just hung in here, I knew she'd let go. I wasn't letting up until she came. I wanted her happy and boneless before I entered her for the first time.

In a delicious minute, she exhaled a moan, then her body clenched all around my fingers, and she began to quake.

She was exceedingly lovely when she orgasmed. Her brown eyes fluttered open, and her hair flew all over the place. Her slim pale legs splayed across the bed.

Soon, I could tell she got overly-sensitive, and I slowed.

"Hey," I whispered, and kissed her.

"That felt soooo—" She didn't finish her sentence. Her smile was sated.

But not sated enough.

"You ready for more?"

She nodded vigorously.

I got off the bed and grabbed a condom out of my bag. My hands shook as I ripped it open and sheathed myself. Prowling back to the bed, I hovered over her as she separated her legs, and I settled in between them. Ready to connect with her this way for the first time ever.

"C'mon," she said. "I love you, Tate. I want to do this with you."

"I love you, too," I said.

She pulled me down and helped me line up to enter her. And then oh so slowly, I pushed in.

Then I looked up at her and gasped.

We were joined together, and I was overwhelmed with love and devotion and the feeling because oh, fuck. This was *unnnngggghhh* so good.

I stayed still, although all I wanted to do was move.

Her warmth surrounded me, and she squeezed me tightly, and my eyes rolled back into the back of my head. Then I came to. "You okay, honey?"

She nodded. "Fine. I'm totally fine." Then she gave me a broad smile. "Actually, it feels special."

"It does," I whispered.

I tried going slowly, but with her heels on my ass, she urged me faster and faster. "You can go faster."

"Not without you coming."

"You already took care of me, Tate. Now it's your turn. Let me take care of you."

I nodded and started thrusting for real. I did my best to focus on her, on her pleasure, but she was goading me on to focus on mine, and it was hard not to when it felt this way.

"God," I grunted. "Why didn't we do this before?"

But that wasn't a real complaint.

I could feel that tingling feeling—the tensing in my body, and I pulled out.

"What?" she whined. "You were going to come."

"Yeah, but you weren't. We can't have that."

I helped her up and then turned her over to her hands and knees, then reached around and started fingering her clit again as I entered her.

She moaned. "That's more like it," I growled.

The change of position had given me a chance to calm, and I focused on my task. Letting her wring as much pleasure out of me as she could. I had one hand on her pussy and the other on a breast, kneading it, and we were molded together, the angle of my dick hitting somewhere deep inside her.

I'd never felt anything that combined the physical and the emotional, the base and the sublime, and so much love and trust between us.

Then I felt it. She started quaking, and her walls started spasming, and it triggered my orgasm, and I came with a roar like a freight train.

Holy fuck.

Aftershocks throbbed through me. My brain was nothing but white noise.

I collapsed onto her back, panting, then rolled over, careful with the condom. At least I remembered to do that.

"We need to do that again," she whispered.

"Yeah," I said. "We do. You're incredible."

"It felt right."

I kissed her. "Just because we're young doesn't mean we don't know what we're doing. I know I love you and will love you for the rest of my life."

And I held her in my arms the whole night.

EPILOGUE

TAP THAT

Audrey

A disembodied voice announced, "Next stop. Fifty-Ninth Street-Lexington Avenue."

"C'mon," Tate said, pulling me to my feet from where I sat on the moving subway train. "This is our stop."

With my hand in his, I got to my feet and went willingly, making my way around the various people sitting and standing in the car. Once I stood in front of the doors, he wrapped his arms around my waist, nuzzling his nose against my neck. Our bodies swayed, waiting for the cars to stop. He planted a kiss on the top of my head, inhaling deeply.

"Did you just smell my hair?" I asked, my tone playful rather than accusatory.

"Yep."

I laughed at how cool he was, and I loved our easy affection. I loved *him*.

With a squeal, the train stopped and the doors parted in front of us.

"Will you tell me where we're going?" I asked, as we

stepped onto the platform, looking around for the entrance. I pulled my cream-colored beanie out of my pocket and put it on my head.

He grinned. "Nope. But you'll figure it out soon enough."

Hand in hand, we followed the subway hordes of New York City to the street above.

While I'd spent plenty of time in San Francisco, New York City was nothing like that familiar foggy city. Older, bigger, with more going on, I'd been walking around Manhattan like a kid in a candy shop for the past few days.

This was just the beginning of our gap year world tour. But Tate wouldn't tell me where we were going next. Only that we were going to do as many things on his list as possible.

Tate had asked if I wanted to go here for the first stop on our Anti-Bucket List, and I easily said yes. Yesterday, he took me to F.A.O. Schwartz, and I bought an auburn-haired Barbie that looked kind of like me.

I cried. I cry a lot these days, but it feels like a relief rather than something to suppress. I'm letting him see all of me, not just the easy things.

Now we headed past Bloomingdale's. Although apparently it wasn't our destination, Tate didn't hurry me. The stores in Manhattan were bigger and just plain old *more* than the ones back home, and we spent time soaking in the atmosphere and inspecting the window displays. On his mom's suggestion, I'd packed an empty bag, and Tate and I'd had more fun buying me the tweedy clothes I loved.

Yesterday, we'd spent the day at Columbia and FIT, checking in with the registrar about our deferred admissions. No problem whatsoever. Walking around the campuses, I just got more and more excited. I knew we had something to look forward to after our gap year. We also scoped out neighborhoods to live in.

It was a late fall day, the perfect kind where you needed a jacket and hat, because those were the best looking. Tate looked particularly handsome in a dark blue stocking cap and a black pea coat.

We crossed the street away from Bloomingdale's, and I got a glimpse of where he was taking me.

"Dylan's Candy Bar?"

He pulled me into his arms. "For my girl who has had all the candy in the world, I thought you might have added this to the list if you'd known about it."

This boy knew me well. I leaned up on my tippy toes and kissed him, because he was the most thoughtful person on the planet.

Except when he liked to squeeze my boobs.

But that was apparently a guy thing, Wren told me.

After kissing him, I dragged him down the street as he laughed, headed straight into the biggest, brightest, most joyful candy shop I'd ever seen.

When I stepped inside the rainbow world of color and sugar, I inhaled deeply. "This place is my heaven."

Instead of answering, Tate just watched me, amused, as I took my time inspecting and cooing over every single display and type of candy. The happier I was, the happier he got.

He was *such* a keeper.

"I think you should pick out anything that strikes your fancy," he said.

That phrase stopped me from my inspection of imported European chocolate. "Strikes my fancy? Who are you, William Randolph Hearst? You gonna build me a castle as a flight of fancy?"

"If you put it down on the list—"

I held up my hand. "No. No castles. I will visit ones with you, but I don't want to live in one."

"You sure?"

The thing with Tate was I couldn't tell if he was kidding or not. Knowing him, he'd do his best to make anything happen. So I had to make this clear. "Yes. Because the more time and money we spend on castles, the less time we have to spend on trains."

He pulled out his phone and the Google doc. "I'm gonna add 'castle' to the ABL, just in case."

"ABL?"

"Anti-Bucket List."

"You're impossible," I said, rolling my eyes, which made him smile.

"I believe you mean, 'handsome.'" Tate's grin went wicked.

"Is he ever, sister," called a little old lady behind me. "You should tap that."

"Oh, trust me," I said, squeezing Tate's hand. "I do."

"Should we FaceTime your mom?" Tate asked, as we entered the hotel lobby, carrying a few bags of candy.

I looked at the time. "Yes, it's perfect. She'll be back from therapy and wanting to chat." I called her.

"Mom!"

"Audrey! Tate! How are you two?"

"Mom, this place is amazing. I think absolutely everything happens in New York City. The energy here is alive. It's far from sleepy Merlot. And yet, being from there interests everyone, since they think I know something about wine."

"Do you burst their bubble and tell them you hate wine?"

"What makes you think I still hate wine?"

"Do you?" She asked accusingly.

"I do. No wine for me."

She laughed. And while she sounded tired, she was also there. Familiar.

After talking to my mom, we rummaged through the bag of candy. I found a pack of gum and unwrapped a piece, popping it in my mouth.

"I feel like I should thank Jade," I said. "She forced me to talk to you sooner. But every time I go to text her, it sounds like I'm being sarcastic or rubbing it in."

"That's nice of you. Nicer than me."

"By being a bitch, she got us together for real. She changed our lives."

"True," he said. "Well, maybe we send her a gift at Penn?"

"Nah. We'll just thank her the next time we see her."

"Sounds good. Here's where we're going next," he said. And he showed me our tickets to Heathrow.

"London?"

"I think we have a pair of sparkly Doc Martens to buy."

"We're going shoe shopping in London?"

"Yep. And for the rest of our lives."

I kissed him, even though I still chewed gum.

And when we were done, somehow the gum wasn't in my mouth anymore.

Grinning, he popped the bubble.

ABOUT THE AUTHOR

Leslie McAdam is a California girl who loves romance and well-defined abs. She lives in a drafty old farmhouse on a small orange tree farm in Southern California with her husband and two small children. Leslie's first published book, The Sun and the Moon, won a 2015 Watty, which is the world's largest online writing competition. She's gone on to receive additional literary awards and has been featured in multiple publications, including Cosmopolitan.com. Her books have been Top 100 Bestsellers on both Amazon and Apple Books. Leslie is employed by day but spends her nights writing about the men of your fantasies.

Website | Facebook group | Tumblr | Wattpad | Book and Main Bites | Quora | Medium

ACKNOWLEDGMENTS

Thanks to:
    Sierra
    Mary
    Kristy
    Heather
    Katy
    Lex
    Jerica
    Deb
    Phala
    Julia
    My family
    Oh, and Lori and Brian, who inspired the story. It's fiction though.

www.ingramcontent.com/pod-product-compliance
Lightning Source LLC
Chambersburg PA
CBHW071919220626
47052CB00002B/416